ELIZABETH POWER

Terms of Possession

Harlequin Books

TORONTO • NEW YORK • LONDON
AMSTERDAM • PARIS • SYDNEY • HAMBURG
STOCKHOLM • ATHENS • TOKYO • MILAN
MADRID • WARSAW • BUDAPEST • AUCKLAND

To Dad and Lyn—
and the fond memory of our day in Bath
With love

ISBN 0-373-11838-4

TERMS OF POSSESSION

First North American Publication 1996.

CHAPTER ONE

IGNORING the anxious green eyes, the tense features in the softly lit mirror, Nadine got up from the dressing-table, feeling the apricot satin nightdress move with disturbing sensuality against her skin.

Whichever way one looked at it, it was still adultery, she thought with an apprehensive little shiver. What other way was there to describe having sex with a married man?

Heat washed over her as she gazed out of the diamond-paned window, down on to the pleasingly lit gardens of the small country hotel. How discreet of him to bring her here, away from London, she reflected, with increasing tension licking through her as she heard water running out of the basin in the adjoining room. Surely one of the West End hotels might have proved a more appropriate setting—a more impersonal place for the cold, meaningless act they were about to——

'Savouring the view?'

The deep, impartial voice jerked her head round in a blaze of rich auburn, her body stiffening from the sudden, stark exposure to that speculative masculine gaze. The satin nightie did nothing to conceal the gentle curves of her body, and feeling the heat of that gaze, with a dryness in her throat, she uttered challengingly, 'Are you?'

He smiled a tight smile—the type she had seen him use often in open court. Cameron Hunter. Brilliant barrister. Ruthless adversary. And Lisa's husband. She had to remember that. Keep reminding herself of the reason why she was here.

'It's commendable,' he approved with a detached softness as he came towards her, a more relaxed smile easing the austerity of hard, strongly defined features.

He hadn't undressed yet, and the pull of something frighteningly basic overrode her relief. Jacketless, he was still wearing the white shirt and dark trousers he had worn at dinner, but his muscular leanness was all too apparent now, and with a tight contraction of her throat she noticed how the black wavy hair curling over his collar was mirrored in the open 'V' of the shirt he had casually loosened.

'I'm sorry if I kept you. I thought you'd be in bed.'

Nadine swallowed, unable to look at that enormous feature of the plushly Victorian room with all it implied.

'No. That's all right. I mean . . .' How could he appear so cool? 'I—I mean . . . you didn't.'

Heaven! She was twenty-four, for goodness' sake! Why did she have to sound like a stammering schoolgirl in contrast with him? Because she didn't have a clue how to handle this situation—never dreaming, when she had originally agreed to the surrogacy arrangements, that it would ultimately come to this.

And he was shrewd enough to realise it, she despaired, seeing the line furrowing the high forehead even before he said, 'Are you sure you . . . really want to go through with this?'

She looked at him quickly. No, she wasn't. Oh, not that his child wasn't the one thing in the world that she dearly wanted! But not like this, she thought—not in these circumstances. She wondered, from his query alone, if he had reservations too.

'To have a child for another woman is a tall order,' he stated phlegmatically. 'You could be forgiven for backing out.'

Backing out? Nadine's body went rigid. Hadn't she considered the consequences of that ever since she had agreed to Lisa's crazy suggestion? Lisa, who had everything except the one thing she desperately longed for—Cameron's child. But she, Nadine, *had* agreed—agreed because the only man she had ever wanted was Cameron Hunter.

Too shy to let him know of her feelings four years ago, she'd had to stand by and painfully watch while he married her best friend—even though she'd always felt that Lisa wasn't really right for him. Therefore the thought of bearing his child—the child Lisa had craved and which, after countless tests, she had ruefully admitted to Nadine she was physically unable ever to give him—seemed like compensation, in a way, for her own loss.

And besides, coming when it had, Lisa's suggestion had been like the answer to a prayer. Nadine had needed money. Money to pay for the vital heart surgery that could save her mother's life.

But the complicated procedure of insemination, with its various tests and no guarantee at the end of it all of success, had all been considered too time-consuming—and time was running out. So really what choice had she had?

'No.' Glad that he had preferred to keep it a totally private affair, and with a steely determination, she lifted her small chin, resolve in every taut line of her fine bone-structure. 'When I enter into a contract—even if it's only a verbal one—I honour it.'

Cameron's mouth took on the barest curve. A disciplined mouth, she had always thought, that could disarm or slay with a single movement. And then every nerve seemed to pulse into violent life as, slipping a hand under the rich sheen of her hair at the nape of her neck, he whispered, 'I'm pleased to hear it,' and drew her face purposefully towards his.

'Cameron...'

'Hush.' The gentle touch of his lips silenced her uncertain murmur, causing her blood to pump with dizzying force along her veins. Their bodies weren't actually touching, but the rough texture of his cheek with the subtle scent of his cologne and the slow brush of his mouth over hers sent such a shiver of sensuality through her that she stiffened in unconscious withdrawal. He was Lisa's husband! She had no right...

'Relax.'

Of course. He could tell. Nothing would escape him. He was trained to observe and detect every small flinch, every weakness in the human character.

'I'm sorry.' She closed her eyes to blot out the sight of his tall, wholly masculine figure as he pushed back the auburn waves from her shoulder, his dark head inclining to the bare flesh he had exposed.

Nadine sucked in her breath. Dear God, how long had she wanted this? 'Cameron, I...' Her breath shuddered through her lungs, making her voice sound provocatively husky. 'I mean...' Oh, goodness! Was this really happening? 'I thought...' What had she thought? That it would be quick and emotionless—at least on his part? Not this dangerously gentle seduction that was threatening to liberate the futile emotions she had nursed for him since she was eighteen and which she had bound in iron fetters the day he had married Lisa. 'Couldn't we just...?'

His laugh was a soft rumble in his throat. 'We could,' he murmured silkily, trailing kisses along the smooth line of her throat to the lobe of her ear. 'But you wouldn't thank me for that.'

No, she thought, clenching her hands at her sides to stem the shocking tide of prohibited pleasure that ran through her as his tongue found the sensitive inner curve of her ear. At thirty-four, he would know women well—and the effect he had upon them without even trying.

'You're trembling.' His hands were resting on her shoulders, strong and firm. 'I know the circumstances of this...arrangement might be a bit unusual, but you're not a child. Being in this situation with a man——' his chin lifted to embrace the sensuously lit bedroom '—surely can't be entirely foreign to you?'

Nadine gulped. If only he knew! 'No,' she lied, unable to tell him just how inexperienced she was—that she'd never met another man who had interested her beyond anything even mildly physical since the day he'd stormed into her office during her first week in his chambers all those years ago and castigated her for an incompetence that hadn't been her fault. And at that moment she envied his confident maturity, his sexual sophistication that far exceeded her own.

Nevertheless, she still wasn't prepared for the extent of her own startling reaction as he suddenly pulled her against him, for her body's shocking response to the hard warmth of him through her nightdress, to the sudden firm demands of his mouth.

Sensations shook her, her knees seeming to liquefy so that her hands slid to his shoulders and clung to him, to the solidity of warm muscle beneath the soft sensuality of his shirt.

How many nights had she lain awake as a hapless teenager, stifling her feverish longing for this in the dark oblivion of her pillow? How many times since had she discouraged male interest beyond anything further than the odd innocent kiss, finding all potential suitors lacking the dangerous and exciting dynamism of this one man?

His arms were tightening like a vice around her so that she could feel every hard, aroused sinew of his body. She shuddered with the sensations she was fighting to control, wrought with the almost unbearable exertion of self-restraint.

How could she allow herself to feel like this? To forget that he was married—married to Lisa! She tensed, groaning a soft protest, and through her swimming senses heard him say, 'Come on, Nadine. Loosen up. It's only you and me.'

And for you it's just a business arrangement, she thought, stifling the silent despair in her heart by telling herself rather unconvincingly that she was doing this solely to help her mother.

'It's all right for you. I...' How could she tell him that she didn't wholly know what was expected of her? That she was afraid to let herself go, because if she did then he might guess just how she felt about him?

'Leave it to me, Nadine.'

Almost as if he had read her mind he was taking command, and she caught her breath as he suddenly lifted her easily and carried her over to the bed.

His hands, burning through the apricot satin, were like flames to dry kindling, and she had to bite her bottom lip to stem a cry at their pleasuring warmth. He was a master at this, she thought hazily as those hands shaped her feminine softness, her breath coming shallowly as he suddenly slipped the thin straps off her shoulders, drew her nightdress down over the creamier satin of her breasts.

'You're lovely.' His whispered appreciation of her showed in the taut lines of his face, and she closed her eyes to the deepening blue of his.

She could hear the ragged quality of his breathing, feel the hardening of his body as he lay across her, his lips burning over the soft, creamy rise of her breasts.

He was aroused, she thought, tensing. And—dear heaven—so was she. And yet... Beads of perspiration broke out across her forehead, along the perfect top line of her mouth. He was a man. It was his prerogative to enjoy a woman. But if she expressed the same pleasure...

'It'll be easier if you relax.'

Of course, he knew. There was an impatient edge to the deep voice as he moved away from her, and she didn't need to open her eyes to realise that he was shrugging out of his clothes. Yet how could she do as he was suggesting without giving herself away? Or, worse, making him think that she was entirely wanton?

When he came back to her, though, peeling the last barrier of satin from her body, the touch of his warm flesh against hers was like an electric charge to her senses, and she stifled a gasp, jaw clenched against the sweetness piercing her lower body, as he suddenly dipped his head to her breast.

'Oh, please...' It came out as a shuddering protest against the insidiously sweet torture of his mouth.

Eyes shuttered, hair spread like fiery silk across the pillow, she waited tensely as he moved. If only he would end it now—get it over with before her body betrayed her...

'Look at me.'

His imperative tone broke through her silent struggle. His eyes were a deep, inky blue. His usually groomed hair was ruffled, his features impassioned, and the skin over those prominent cheekbones was taut, flushed with need.

'Are you always so uptight when you're making love? What does a man have to do to relax you? Show me what you want.' His voice seemed to shudder from within the deep wall of his chest. 'What is it you want? Show me, Nadine.'

You! She censored the thought from her brain before it could take shape. She had no right to think it! No right at all! But the burn of his lips across the flat plane of her stomach and the deep persuasion of his voice were robbing her of her last vestige of control. Her need seemed to explode inside her, shattering her restraint into fragments, galvanising her into a sobbing, writhing surrender that she couldn't have kept from him any longer any more than she could have flown.

I'm sorry, Lisa! The thought was blown away like dust in the wind as she succumbed to the forces of a passion matched only by the force and power of the man who was suddenly moving, claiming her, unlocking the mysteries of her body.

Desire swamped her like a violent storm so that she knew only a sweet pleasure and a sudden pain—pain, brief and sharp—before the consuming, spiralling ecstasy of his possession.

When he rolled away from her some time afterwards, got up without saying a word, Nadine eased herself up on an elbow, half-afraid to look at him. Was he angry? Shocked—as she was—by that tempestuous and involuntary response?

The soft lights from the dressing-table threw a warm glow over his magnificent nakedness and she glanced away, embarrassed by her shameless surrender to it as he shrugged into a white towelling robe.

'Why didn't you tell me you were ... That I'd be the first?' He sounded puzzled, mildly censuring.

'I didn't think it was important,' she responded, with a little shrug. She couldn't tell him that she had been embarrassed about that, too.

'Maybe not to anyone else, but I would have thought where you were concerned it might have been.'

His eyes were hard and penetrating. Trying to see through her, she thought shudderingly, suddenly vibrantly conscious of how she must look in the aftermath of their lovemaking—skin flushed and dewy, hair wild and damp with perspiration. But at least he didn't appear to have guessed the truth.

'What makes a girl sacrifice something so rare and precious simply for money? And don't tell me it wasn't, because if that was the case you'd probably have relinquished it long ago.'

Nadine's shoulders stiffened. 'That's insulting.'

'It wasn't meant to be.'

'No?' Her chin came up, nostrils dilated with wounded anger. She couldn't forget how opposed he had been to Lisa's suggestion of surrogate motherhood in the beginning. Lisa had had to beg him until he'd finally given in. She wasn't sure, but she guessed what he probably thought about women who accepted payment in exchange for a child—about her, Nadine Kendall—and that frenzied response to him just now wouldn't have helped to change his opinion in any way.

'What I mean is that you're a very beautiful girl.' He opened the mini-fridge, took out a bottle of chilled water. 'Don't try and tell me that a lot of men haven't tried to seduce you.'

'No... I mean ... some.'

So he wasn't immune to her femininity, even if he had always displayed no more than a cool imperviousness towards her. After all, she was Lisa's friend, not his. As for involvements, even if she *had* met a man who had been able to rid her of this mindless infatuation with Cameron, she would have had no desire to rush into one with her eyes closed. A serious relationship—which was all she would settle for—needed to be right. She'd seen from the break-up of her parents' marriage how devastating and painful a mistake could be.

She heard the still water tumble into a glass, her gaze following the strong line of his throat as he took a long draught before offering her some. She shook her head.

'The main reasons for sacrificing one's virginity are usually love, passion, or just plain and simple curiosity. So what makes you different, Nadine? Why has the importance of money suddenly triumphed over the other three?'

His gaze was too intense and she looked away, like a witness with a guilty secret to hide, plagued not only by her reckless emotions but also by the memory of her mother's pinched features, her laboured breathing; by her desperate plea when she'd failed to talk Nadine out of paying for her treatment.

'Don't tell anyone what I'm having done—how serious this is. I couldn't bear to be thought of as an invalid.'

She ventured a look at Cameron. He had a reputation in court for being pitiless. Yet even *he* would feel some, she thought, if she told him about the heart condition that was threatening her mother's life. Only a by-pass operation could offer her the chance of recovery, but the scheduled surgery had been postponed because of the ever-increasing cut-backs in the Health Service, and Nadine had had to watch, helpless, as her mother's health gradually deteriorated, aware that even the simplest task now made her breathless and fatigued.

Yes, somehow she felt he'd understand. Only she couldn't go back on the promise she had made to her mother. And not only that, Lisa had been her friend since childhood—had known both her parents—and if it ever got back to Dawn Kendall how she, Nadine, was financing her forthcoming operation . . .

Inwardly, she shuddered. Even with the payment Cameron had already made to her she'd met enough maternal objection when she'd let her mother believe she was simply using her savings to help meet the hospital's fees. But if she ever discovered the truth...

'Does there have to be a reason, m'lud?' she parried lightly in response to his query about sacrificing herself. And in a desperate bid to keep her secret—change the subject—with a nervous little laugh she uttered flippantly, 'Any more questions for the defence?'

Those shrewd eyes narrowed speculatively as he put down his glass. 'I'm not a lord.' Unpretentiously he drew attention to the way she had addressed him. 'And certainly not a judge—yours or anybody else's.'

But he was, she thought, sensing the assessment going on inside that brilliant brain. Fear was leaping through her—fear of another shaming submission and of the threat to her emotions that she neither wanted nor welcomed—as he slipped off his robe and, sliding back into bed with her, said with meaningful softness, 'And no, there'll be no more questions.'

Unusually edgy, Nadine started as the phone rang in the little Dickensian office.

'Hi! It's me. I thought I'd be back earlier than this but the car had other ideas.'

Nadine smiled, relaxing at the sound of her boss's friendly voice. Recently qualified, Larry Lawson had joined the firm two years after she had, when her old boss had retired, and he promised to be a brilliant solicitor provided he kept a rather rebellious streak in check.

'How's your mother? Is she better?'

She had told him on Friday that she was spending the weekend with her mother as she wasn't too well, but she had refrained from mentioning either the fact that she had spent those two days by her mother's bedside in a private south coast hospital, or the vital surgery the woman had undergone during the previous week.

'She'll be OK,' she responded, her chest tightening painfully as she said it. If only she could be sure!

'In that case, could you prepare that brief I dictated to counsel as soon as you can? Thinking of which, I saw the man in action in court this morning—you know, that Laser v Brompton case? Holy mackerel! He isn't called Hunter for nothing—the way that man hounds after the truth! It looks as though *she* might have been lying all the way through the proceedings, and if she has—heaven help her! He'll make mincemeat of her!'

A sensation shivered through Nadine beneath the chic blue pin-striped suit. As he had done with her? Oh, not with that same skill of ruthless intellect for which he was renowned, but sensually, through a total devastation of her senses. Because he had made love to her again, several times during that pre-arranged weekend together, silently and clinically, without words, while she, after that first shameful loss of control, had been unable to withhold the response he'd so easily wrung from her.

And when he had driven her home at the end of that weekend he had seemed more aloof and remote from her than he had ever done, when she had wanted...what? Affection from him? No, of course not! she assured herself with biting self-castigation. He was another woman's husband. Therefore, what right had she to feel so stupidly hurt and alone?

'Hello? Are you still there?'

'Yes...yes, I am.' She had forgotten Larry on just hearing Cameron's name. And that was wrong, a strong sense of integrity served to remind her. But she hadn't seen or heard from him since that weekend, and that was nearly four weeks ago now. 'I'd better ring off. I'm expecting another call,' she advised a little tensely, omitting to add that what she was waiting for was the result of the test she had had done last week. When the phone rang again, the instant she put it down, she almost leapt out of her chair.

Her fingers were still trembling five minutes later as they picked out Lisa's home number, her heart thudding, her thoughts chaotically numb. She had been praying she would be pregnant. She didn't think she could take an assault on her senses by Cameron Hunter a second time without disastrous consequences to her emotions, though he had managed to remain entirely detached and uncommitted. And now...

'Lisa?' She took a deep breath and gave her friend the news.

'Wow! What a stud I'm married to! He certainly didn't waste any time with you, did he?' Lisa responded—rather indelicately, Nadine thought, in the circumstances, though her friend sounded delighted enough. 'So you'll have the baby... I must admit that's the only worry I would have had about carrying if I *had* been able to conceive—the fear of blowing up like a balloon and staying like it for ever afterwards.' Lisa laughed, reminding Nadine of her friend's constant battle to keep a check on her rather curvy figure. 'I'll get everything arranged. Nursery, nanny, toys, soundproof room. Only joking!' she added quickly. 'I might even decide to stay home and play full-time mother.'

Lisa was twenty-seven, three years older than herself, and had worked as a legal executive in the same law practice, which was how she, Nadine, had come to hear about the secretarial vacancy in the first place. At the time she had welcomed the move away from the man who was occupying too much of her thoughts and who was scarcely aware of her existence, fearing that her own violent crush on him was in danger of prejudicing her work.

It was Lisa who had brought him back into her life after meeting him at a party; Lisa who had been just as hopelessly ensnared by the terrifying strength of his attraction. After that he'd sometimes come into the office, or call at Lisa's while Nadine was there. He'd been aloof, yet somehow more indulgent towards her then than when she had been working with him, little knowing how his lethal sexuality was affecting her as he watched her blossoming into full womanhood.

Sometimes, when he had smiled at her, it had been as if the earth was tipping off its axis. Indeed, the responses rocketing through her had been so profound she had deluded herself that he had to be feeling something too. But it was Lisa he had married so suddenly and unexpectedly four years ago; Lisa who had stayed on with the firm as an unwitting yet constant reminder of all Nadine had lost, with her bubbling happiness and her ceaseless fervour for him. She had only left on her doctor's advice—rather futile, as it had turned out—that less pressure of work might bring her the child she wanted.

'Am I the first to know? Oh, great!' Having forced herself back to the present, Nadine could almost feel her friend's joy. 'Then let *me* tell Cameron. It'll be as though I'm having this baby myself!'

Wistfully Nadine smiled. She could understand how Lisa felt. But her own emotions seemed numbed—strangely shell-shocked—as though she hadn't yet begun again to feel.

'You were certainly worth every cent, Nadine, so now you can go out and blow it! Plus you've had the added bonus of knowing what it's like to sleep with Cameron Hunter!'

'Lisa!' Nadine felt hot colour invading her cheeks. She didn't want to think about that. Nor could she tell her friend about her mother's operation, and the expensive after-care on which the money was being spent.

'Oh, come on, don't be coy about it. I know you must have been simply dying to! If you aren't admitting to it, then you're the only one of my friends who hasn't. But it does have its disadvantages, I can assure you now. As far as any other man's concerned, you'll be spoilt for life!'

Embarrassed, Nadine laughed awkwardly. Didn't she already know that? 'Be seeing you, Lisa,' she said quickly, winding up the conversation and putting down the phone, wondering suddenly if Lisa had been drinking.

*   *   *

She was watching the end of a gripping thriller when the telephone rang that evening, the lateness of the hour making her heart lurch apprehensively as she crossed the small sitting room and switched off the television set to answer it. Supposing it was the hospital?

'Nadine?' The last thing she had expected to hear was Cameron Hunter's deep voice. 'Nadine, you sound worried. Are you all right?'

'Yes. Yes, I'm fine.' Hastily she pulled herself together. If she wanted to keep her troubles from anyone, it was him.

'I believe congratulations are in order. Lisa told me. Any problems? Or are you feeling all right?'

Funny that he should be the one to ask that, she thought, because Lisa hadn't.

'No, none,' she assured him, even if her knees did feel like jelly! And not only, she realised shamefully, from the dread of bad news about her mother.

'You sound breathless. I hope I didn't get you out of bed.' There was more than courteous concern behind that remark.

'No, you didn't.' Pique turned her cheeks to flame. She might be just a convenient womb for his child but he did, after all, have exclusive knowledge of her sleeping habits, and therefore shouldn't have had the audacity to suggest anything else!

'Good.' Was that double-edged too? She wasn't sure. 'I merely wanted you to know that I intend to see that you get all the necessary care and assistance you need over the next eight months or so. I'll have your medical fees taken care of.' As he—albeit unwittingly—had made it possible for her to take care of her mother's? 'Any problems, ring me . . . or Lisa.'

'Thanks.' She wasn't sure whether she had imagined that slight hesitancy in his voice. He sounded so coldly practical, though, as though he were simply dealing with one of his clients. But then that was all this was to him, wasn't it? she thought poignantly. A business transaction. Even so, an unexpected wave of loneliness washed over her after he had rung off, so crushing that she found herself giving in to a sudden bout of tears, which she tried to justify as only the result of her condition coupled with the worries about her mother.

Days tumbled into a week, then two, during which Nadine arranged for her mother's convalescence in a private nursing home nearer London, where she could receive the necessary care as well as the cardiac rehabilitation she needed at the nearby hospital—although Nadine was concerned to hear that her recovery was being impeded by a slight cold.

'You're looking downcast today,' Larry remarked one morning, coming into Nadine's office and catching her sitting at her desk in one of her anxious reveries. 'What do I have to do to whip up a smile on that lovely face?' And, with mischief in his eyes, 'Ever been beaten with a will?'

Nadine ducked to avoid the rolled white parchment he was brandishing, his jocular play on words producing the desired effect.

'You'll never endear yourself to our senior partner,' she chided laughingly. Beneath a wild mat of curly brown hair an ear-ring, she noticed, had made itself evident since the previous day.

'Thank goodness for that!' Larry laid a hand on his heart. 'He's not my type. But while we're on the subject of being clobbered, you'll be interested to know Hunter won that case for us—hot on the heels of his success with the Laser-Brompton affair. He must be every opponent's nightmare. You should go and watch him handling a case some time, if you haven't done so yet.'

A rush of nausea engulfed her, piercingly acute, and as she staggered to her feet to try and make it to the Ladies' she heard Larry's voice coming anxiously, distantly, behind her. 'Gosh! You look ghastly! Are you all right?'

She was, eventually, and refused his advice to go home as well as his invitation to lunch.

'Perhaps you had better go easy on the rations with an upset tum,' he accepted, his obvious concern making her feel guilty in having led him to believe that that was all it was.

She felt better after grabbing a quick sandwich in town, but there was one problem worrying her that she had to straighten out with herself, once and for all.

Strong as her crush on Cameron Hunter had been as a teenager, she had been brutally forced to mature after he had married Lisa, resigning herself to the fact that he belonged to someone else. But ever since that weekend, when he had taken her to that hotel, those old feelings for him had returned with frightening tenacity, making her heart pound every time she heard his name, her temperature rise every time she thought about the mind-blowing skill in the way he had made love to her. And that was both stupid and ill-advisable, she warned herself chasteningly. She had to gain control of herself— strive for the detached and adult attitude in all this that he was obviously managing to maintain.

However, fate, it seemed, was out to test her that day, she decided when, having bought a few things in one of the department stores, she suddenly found herself taking a detour through the mother and baby department.

How strange that she should find herself looking at this, she thought, hesitantly fingering a small white matinée jacket that was hanging on a rail.

When the three of them had talked about this baby in the beginning, Lisa had said she would want to keep the facts of its birth a secret from it, but Cameron had insisted that every child had a right to the truth about its origins. But how would her child feel when it asked its parents, 'What happened to my real mother?' How would it react to them saying, 'She gave you up for cash.'

No! The negation was so strong that she thought she had spoken it aloud. She was being silly. Her baby was going to have loving parents, a far more comfortable and privileged existence than any she could provide. And it wouldn't have reason to think too harshly of her, surely—even if it didn't realise it, it had been conceived so that its own grandmother might have the chance to live.

She turned away from the coat, but there were other things to torment her. Little jumpsuits. Rattles. Cuddly toys.

God! She needed a deep breath to stem the acute emotion that suddenly welled up inside her. She hadn't reckoned on so much feeling so soon. And supposing Mum didn't...

She couldn't bring herself to form the thought in her mind. But this was Dawn Kendall's grandchild she was carrying. Part of her mother. Part of herself. Perhaps the only blood relative she might have one day. Would she be strong enough when the time came simply to hand it over?

Determinedly she got a grip on her recalcitrant emotions, urging herself away from the baby department. Regardless of her own feelings, and the way she felt about the child's father, she had entered into an agreement— had accepted money in part-payment under that agreement as well as giving Lisa the promise of hope in her childless marriage. She would—had to—remain detached.

Therefore, she decided, it would be best to avoid any further excursions into town by herself.

So when Larry rang her at the flat the following morning and invited her to go swimming with him during the lunch-break, happily she agreed, packing a swimsuit in her bag before she left for the office.

'Very nice,' he approved that lunchtime, when she surfaced from under the chlorinated blue water at the sports centre. Her pregnancy hadn't yet begun to show, although the initial changes in her body had given a firm roundness to her breasts beneath the emerald satin of her swimsuit, temporarily giving her the voluptuous figure she had always envied Lisa. 'Ever thought of getting involved with an up-and-coming solicitor?'

Larry's eyes continued to appraise her, his dark hair plastered to his head. 'Good prospects. Good sense of humour. And an immediate discount on any legal fees.' He grinned.

'Only if I can wear the ear-rings!' Nadine teased, swimming away, because she knew Larry wasn't really serious. At least, she hoped he wasn't! Larry Lawson was certainly too unconventional for her!

She was walking back with him through the car park when she noticed the small white BMW convertible parked a little distance away, recognised the cerise silk blouse of the woman sitting in the driving seat.

'It's Lisa!' Nadine hesitated, looking apologetically at the slim, rangy man beside her. 'Would you mind if I just pop over and have a few words? I'll see you in the car.'

She didn't have any special reason for wanting to see Lisa, but she didn't want her friend to drive off without knowing she was there. That was until she drew nearer the car, and then she stopped in her tracks, suddenly feeling rooted to the spot.

It was Lisa, all right. Nadine couldn't fail to recognise the chic, short brown hair, raked through with blonde streaks and hard masculine fingers as her friend gave herself up to the arms of the man who was kissing her so passionately. Only it wasn't Cameron!

Paralysed with shock, for a few moments Nadine couldn't move. Then, gathering her faculties together, not wanting Lisa to see her, she tore blindly back across the car park.

How could she? The question harrowed her along with the nausea that sprang from more than just the early stages of her pregnancy. How *could* she? Lisa and another man?

She caught Larry's surprised, 'You weren't long,' as she climbed into the ancient purring Renault.

And all she could answer was, 'No.' She couldn't believe it! Why would a woman married to a man like Cameron—a woman who had everything—want to...?

'Are you OK?' Larry directed a curious glance at her as he pulled out of the car park.

'Yes,' she answered mechanically. Only she wasn't. Revulsion was sickening her. Revulsion and bewilderment, and the already dawning significance of the situation.

She was having a baby. The baby Lisa wanted. The baby she, Nadine, had thought was going to a loving, stable home with loving parents. But Cameron couldn't know about this! Intuitively she knew he would never have planned a child if he had thought his marriage wasn't one hundred per cent rock-solid, and she could never have believed Lisa would have—until now. But had she ever really known Lisa?

The seatbelt pulled painfully across her breasts as Larry braked behind the car he had been about to overtake.

'Sorry.' He grimaced apologetically. 'This chap in front shouldn't be on the road.'

Nadine forced a wan smile, still deep in the mire of her thoughts about Lisa. Lisa and that other man. She had always known her friend was volatile, perhaps even a little neurotic at times recently, but she had put that down to Lisa's desperation for a baby. And now...

Absently she brushed her damp hair back from her face, staring sightlessly at the busy road ahead. Lisa was deceiving them both—her and Cameron. So how could she, Nadine, hand over her own baby to a woman who was obviously unstable? Deliver it into a home that could wind up broken—just as her own had been?

She scarcely knew what she was doing that afternoon. The decision to which she had come was something that had to be acted upon—and quickly—and her insides were churning queasily as she rang the number of Cameron's chambers.

What was she going to say to him? I need to see you? And if he agreed to her request, what then?

A mixture of contrary emotions ran through her as a feminine voice told her, 'I'm afraid he's still in court. Can I get him to call you when—and if—he comes back?'

'No!' Her insides were tying themselves in knots. She didn't want him ringing her at the office. This matter was too private to risk discussing with anyone else around, apart from which she didn't think she could stand the suspense of waiting for his call.

'I'll try again later,' she volunteered, feeling like a coward, but as she put down the phone she knew she couldn't just sit around hoping for him to come back.

She asked Larry if he'd mind her leaving early, and was relieved when he instantly assumed she was still feeling off-colour from the previous day, which ruled out the need for any further explanations, and within minutes she was on her way to the courts.

Hot, her pulse racing, she nevertheless slipped on her light summer jacket as she entered the great Gothic-style building. A security man searched her bag—along with those of other visitors and tourists—before allowing her in through the awesome grandeur of the main hall.

'Do you know where I'll find Cameron Hunter?' Urgently she asked what looked like a member of court staff, and above the echoing sounds of other voices and general activity he started to say something, just as a more familiar voice spoke from behind.

'Nadine?'

Her breath seemed to lock in her lungs as she swung to face him. Black-gowned, file under his arm, the familiar wig crowning those strong, disciplined features, he looked the intimidating advocate that these days even his more experienced colleagues held in the greatest esteem. That ruthless bearing about him served only to heighten that devastating sexual aura surrounding him.

'What is it?' His shoes made a light tap on the mosaic paving as he came towards her, as austere a figure as his stern forebears, staring down at her from the imposing walls. 'Is anything wrong?'

Nadine swallowed. How could she tell him without incriminating Lisa? How could she explain her decision without giving him a reason why?

'I—I can't keep our agreement.' That wigged forehead creased as though he couldn't quite grasp what she was saying. 'I'm keeping the baby.' It came out too bluntly with the effort of trying to keep her voice steady, and her stomach muscles tightened as Cameron's eyes glittered like dark sapphires.

'You *what*?'

Oh, heaven! What could she say? I love it! And I can't give my baby up to a woman who can't even be faithful to her husband! How could she tell him that without causing serious consequences to his marriage?

'I'm keeping it,' she repeated tremulously, shuddering from the daunting challenge written in every hard line of his face.

'And just what——?'

'Hunter!'

He broke off as someone called to him and as he glanced towards the similarly robed man who was gesturing to him, saying something about seeing the judge, Nadine seized her opportunity and fled.

Oh, what a stupid, stupid thing to do! Breathless, blood racing, she came out into the bright July sunshine, anxiously glancing back over her shoulder with a sigh of relief to realise that Cameron hadn't chased after her. He probably had more pressing business with the judge. But if her decision had angered him, then running away like that would only have incensed him further, she realised dauntingly. Only what else could she have done?

She had no sound explanation to offer for her decision to keep the baby—only the truth. And there was no way that she was going to tell him that! If Lisa was playing around it was hardly *her* business, or her right to bring it to his attention. What *was* her business, though, was making certain that her baby had a secure and happy home. And if that meant having one parent instead of two, as originally planned, then it would have to be.

Still unable to face him, though, when she hadn't yet come to terms with Lisa's betrayal, she went back to the flat, packed a bag, and, worried that he might call, took off for the suburbs to be near her mother for the weekend on the first available train.

When she arrived back late on Sunday night it was with the knowledge that the threatened cold following her mother's operation hadn't developed into anything serious. Consequently it was the memory of Lisa in the car park with that other man which kept her awake for hours. That, and what she herself was going to say to Cameron when he demanded to see her—as he undoubtedly would, she thought, with a cold apprehension stealing through her.

Finally, though, she drifted into a restless slumber, waking with such a severe bout of morning sickness that she had to telephone the office to say she wouldn't be in until later.

It was halfway through the morning before she began to feel better, but her stomach muscles tightened painfully when the doorbell rang just as she was preparing to leave.

'Going somewhere?' Cameron's gaze flitted coldly over her short-sleeved white blouse and beige skirt, and the matching jacket she had thrown over her arm.

'I—I was just leaving for the office.' Looking unusually pale, she took a step back as he thrust his way in uninvited.

'The office can wait.' He threw the door closed behind him, and a contrary mixture of fear and desolation shivered through Nadine. On Friday he'd looked angry. Today he was looking at her with an emotion almost akin to hatred, his voice purposefully soft as he said, 'You aren't going anywhere.'

He seemed big and imposing in her tiny hallway, memory serving to remind her, as her eyes registered the

impeccable cut of his dark suit, that he had never actually been in her flat before.

'You've already had half the morning off. Another
hour isn't going to make any difference—only to the answers you're going to give me!'

Apprehensive, Nadine took another step back, feeling
the sudden cool barrier of the wall through her thin
blouse. So he'd telephoned the office first.

'Cameron—I know you've a right to be angry...'

'Angry?' He gave a harsh laugh. 'Oh, I'm not angry!
I'm downright disgusted!' She gasped as he moved disturbingly close, his hands coming up, one on either side
of her, so that she was imprisoned against the wall. 'You
come and tell me you're going to keep that baby, without
even having the guts to stay and explain why, and then
spend the whole weekend conveniently out of reach—
and probably at my expense!'

'That's not true!' His words cut into her like shards
of jagged glass. His closeness was making her head swim,
evoking feelings—memories—of an intimacy she didn't
want to remember.

'Isn't it?' His mouth was a slash of disdain. 'Then
where the hell were you? I've been ringing—calling round
since you ran out on me on Friday. Where have you
been? In hiding? Afraid to face me, Nadine?' His gaze
raked icily over the tense lines of her face. 'I wonder
why?'

His tone had grown so unnervingly soft that she shuddered visibly. He'd judged her actions correctly, if not
her motives!

'Hasn't a woman the right to want to keep her child?'
she uttered, her green eyes holding his unwaveringly, in
spite of herself. 'It's something that takes over. A maternal instinct...'

'Maternal instincts be hanged!' Tremblingly she shrank
from his palpable anger. 'You'll have to do better than
that, Nadine. And why didn't you tell Lisa? I thought
she and you were supposed to be friends. Why come to
me with your cold-hearted little message? Or did even

the self-centred Nadine Kendall have enough sensitivity to realise that she wouldn't be able to take it?'

She looked at him, scared. Oh, God! Please don't let her actions have done anything to...

'Stop piling on the innocence, Nadine. She was counting on that baby—and you know it! Do you realise the depths of frustration and disappointment she had to go through—the desperation she had to feel to have to resort to asking another woman to provide her with the baby she couldn't conceive herself? And suddenly to be told she wasn't going to have it after all——' She could feel his loathing in the breath that shuddered through his lungs, in the angry, pulsing heat of his body. 'You've broken up my marriage, you mercenary, calculating little bitch! And if you think you're going to rob me of my child as well as wrecking my home, you've got another think coming!'

Nadine stared at him, eyes disbelieving. Lisa—gone? True, she'd seen her in the car park, kissing that other man. But leaving Cameron...

'It wasn't my fault,' she uttered meekly, stunned both by the knowledge that Lisa would actually want to end her marriage and the sudden cold fear that Cameron might try to take the baby away.

'No?' Clearly he wasn't going to accept that, she realised despairingly, feeling a little less threatened when he lowered his arms, slipping his hands into his trouser pockets. 'You think you're blameless?'

'Yes! I mean...' Oh, goodness! What was she trying to say? She'd only been doing what she'd thought was best for the baby—what any mother in the same situation would have done. But if Cameron believed Lisa was so innocent, then let him carry on thinking it! It wasn't her place to put him straight. He'd hardly thank her for it, anyway. 'I'm sorry,' was all she could offer him, rather lamely.

'Sorry?' He rocked back on his heels, contempt in every hard inch of him. 'Are you trying to tell me you didn't have this planned from the very beginning? If

Lisa was right, and you're as anti-men as she had me believe——'

'She said that?'

'She hardly needed to. It's patently obvious.' She barely heard his scathing response, still trying to come to terms with Lisa saying something that was totally untrue. 'You never go out with anyone—not regularly—only the odd, privileged male you might condescend to allow to date you when you're feeling like some masculine company. So how did you go about choosing the father of your baby? Were you looking for a particular kind of pedigree? Or was it the thought of the five-figure cheque that appealed to the virgo intacta?'

The report that rang through the tiny hall was like the crack of a whip. Open-mouthed, hand smarting, Nadine stared at the reddening mark on his cheek, and she gave a small, frightened cry as he grabbed her, pushing her back against the wall.

'Don't you dare raise your hand to me, you cheap, double-crossing little vixen! All that talk about honour!' His hands on her upper arms were bruising, frighteningly powerful, his contemptuous reminder of that night in that Essex hotel scorching her cheeks with shame. 'You used me!'

'That's not true!'

'No?' His fingers tightened relentlessly on her bare flesh. 'You wanted a child without the inconvenience of a husband. But may I remind you that I'm that child's father, and I'll fight you for custody every step of the way?'

Panic filled her eyes and she said desperately, 'You can't make me give it up!'

'Legally, no.' Of course. He knew the law—better than anyone. 'Any more than you can extract any more cash from me if you change your mind and decide to. But if you think you can take my money and keep that baby, then I'll have you know now that I'll have my money's worth out of you in other ways!'

'No!' Her hands came up to try and hold him off when she saw the threatening purpose in his eyes, but he was too strong for her, his body pinning her to the wall, his mouth coming down on hers with angry, humiliating intent.

His lips were punishing, the hands that had been holding her cruelly against him suddenly ripping at the collar of her blouse.

Dear heaven! He thought her no better than a whore! she thought wildly, her senses ravaged by the scent and heat and anger emanating from him, by that angry mouth against her throat, against her shoulder. Only her frenzied 'No!' seemed finally to drag him back to his senses.

Releasing her, and so abruptly that she staggered back against the wall, he turned away from her with a shuddering imprecation, as though he was revolted by her— by himself, for his own loss of control.

'Do what you will,' he snarled, contempt twisting his mouth. 'Go where you will—to the other side of the world if you've a mind to. But I'll find you.' And as he turned to leave, through a blanket of fear and dizzying nausea, she heard his intimidating promise, 'As long as you have my child you'll never be rid of me, Nadine!'

CHAPTER TWO

STIFLED by the heat in the overcrowded train, Nadine stood clinging to the handgrip, praying for her station to emerge through the darkness of the Underground as a wave of sickness washed over her.

What was it they said? That it only lasted three months? Well, roll on three months! she thought wistfully as her stomach lurched with the rolling motion of the train. But what then?

With a little shiver of reluctance she recalled Cameron's resolute promise to her the previous day. Did he intend to fight her for custody eventually, as he'd threatened to do, even without Lisa? Knowing, as he'd already admitted, that he would probably have no chance—or very little—of succeeding? Or did he despise her so much for being—as he believed—instrumental in destroying his marriage, that he intended to make her pay in some other humiliating way?

She fought a cold, queasy fear as she remembered his remark about taking his money's worth, recalled the hostility of his kisses before he had finally gained command of himself again, and she was glad when at last the train whined to a standstill and she was out of the Underground. Although her troubles were only compounded by the news which was waiting for her at the office.

'Larry's gone,' Marion, the junior partner's secretary, came into her tiny office to tell her. 'He had words with our senior early this morning and walked out. I think it was the ear-ring that finally did it.' The young woman offered a sympathising smile. 'I thought I ought to warn you, though...' She hesitated, as though searching for the right words. 'I heard the old man telling

31

the other partners he wouldn't be replacing him... So I don't quite know where that leaves you.'

Redundant, Nadine thought with a despairing grimace. She had her worst fears confirmed within minutes of the other girl's revelation and by that lunchtime she had cleared out her desk and left.

Not that she had been compelled to, she reflected when she was on her way to register with the nearest secretarial agency; they had given her the choice of working until the end of the month. But to avoid awkward questions she had planned to leave anyway, before her pregnancy started to show, and so this way, she decided, was best. At least if she was working for an agency suspicions wouldn't be aroused if her morning sickness sometimes prevented her from getting in some days until after ten!

Fortunate enough to secure a temporary assignment starting the very next day, she found herself working in a very plush insurance office on the other side of town.

She had given the convalescent home the agency's number in case someone should need to contact her urgently. She was disappointed, however, to have received no contact from Lisa, though she had been only half expecting to, nor a mere telephone call from Larry—if only to express regrets over putting her out of a job!

Still, he was probably too busy looking for one himself, she thought wryly, coming out of the modern office with two other girls at the end of the week. Her companions' animated, 'Ooh, what a car! What a man!' coupled with, 'Friend of yours, Nadine?' drew her attention to the gleaming black Mercedes parked at the kerb, whose driver's window was whirring smoothly open.

'Hello, Nadine.' Cameron's smile was coolly reserved. 'Get in. I'll take you home.'

Nadine's hackles rose at his arrogance in assuming that she was going straight home or that she would even step into his car after the way he had treated her the other day. But her colleagues were responding to that supreme masculine confidence in a way that told her they would take him up on his offer if she didn't, and the last thing she wanted was to make a scene in front of them, so reluctantly she obeyed, her senses instantly assailed by the light, evocative scent of his cologne mingling with the expensive leather of his upholstery.

'I'm surprised you haven't got your own transport by now,' was his casual comment after he had reminded her to fasten her seatbelt and was pulling away from the kerb.

What did he mean? That he had paid her well enough to afford to? she thought, and decided to dismiss it, giving him the benefit of the doubt by responding with, 'Driving's a nightmare in London. I don't think it's worth the hassle. Also, it was a choice of running a car or having a decent place to live and I chose the second.'

'A case of priorities?'

She nodded, wondering if he'd ever had to make similar choices. His car was automatic, too, she remembered from last time, trying not to think about that devastating weekend with him as she watched him drive, not needing to change gear, manoeuvring the big car in and out of the rush-hour traffic with an ease that made a mockery of her statement about driving being a nightmare. Instinctively she knew that everything he did would be effortless.

'Why did you leave your job?' For a second that blue gaze lanced across her, piercingly interrogative as it rested on the fine beige cotton of her suit, the rich sheen of her sun-burnished hair. 'Hoping to avoid any unwanted communication with the father of your child? Is a domestic move on the agenda as well?'

'No, it isn't!' A flush washed over Nadine's skin from the scathing quality of his remarks, and just to show him that she wasn't going to be pushed around, she blurted out, 'And what if it were? It's absolutely no business of yours where I live—or how often I change my job. And for your information, Cameron, I happen to have been made redundant!'

Surprise lessened the dark austerity of his profile. 'What happened?'

When she told him, unintentionally allowing disappointment over Larry's failure to contact her to creep into her voice, he said, 'Sounds about par for the course. Larry Lawson's suffering from a severe case of immaturity—rebelling for rebellion's sake against everything that's got him where he is and that he's privileged enough to be part of. He's going to have to do some growing up if he's going to succeed in law.'

'Oh, really?' A fiery wave cascaded over her shoulder as she turned to face him. 'And I suppose you know him well enough to make such profound accusations about him?' she breathed, indignation bringing her leaping rather too readily to her friend's defence.

'Only in so far as the few professional dealings I've had with him. And the fact that he comes from a long line of very competent solicitors. I know his father.'

'You would.'

The obstinate thrust to her lower lip made him smile, the smile more that of a gloating conqueror than an ally. 'What's wrong, Nadine?' His tone was smooth as he changed lanes and started signalling to take a right-hand turning. 'Don't you like it when someone stakes a claim on something that is rightfully theirs?'

He meant the baby, and on a small, desperate note she said, 'It belongs to me as well.'

'Yes.' He ground the word through clenched teeth, as though he regretted having ever laid eyes upon her. 'And as such we'll discuss it. Where you're going to live during the term of your pregnancy. What you're going to do— because like it or not—it *is* my business, and while you're carrying my child you'll do what's best for it, Nadine.'

She watched a black London cab making a U-turn through the busy traffic. Taxis got away with murder, she thought absently, because they had the gall.

'Oh, don't worry, I intend to!' she retorted hotly, despite the sudden clutch of fear in her stomach that with this man there would be no turning round, no going back on anything he'd said.

'Oh, yes, I forgot!' He uttered a harsh, humourless laugh. 'I've provided you with quite a little nest-egg, haven't I?'

'You'll get it back!' she promised vehemently, to herself as well as to Cameron. 'Every last penny!' Secretly, though, she despaired. She owed him a fortune, and from where she was sitting she couldn't see a day when she would ever be out of his debt. 'And as for looking after my baby, I can assure you I'm more than capable.' Quickly she was changing the subject in an attempt to convey responsibility to him. 'I've got a home. A job——'

'For how long?' He cast a disparaging glance at her as they came around the corner. 'Look at you,' he rasped, keenly aware of the pale, pinched look a more than usually bad day of nausea had given to her fine features. 'You look all-in before you start. So what are you planning to do for the next six months? Go haring off to every corner of the city at a moment's notice? Carry on as if you only had yourself to think about? Hardly a very responsible outlook for a woman in your condition. And what happens afterwards? After it's born?'

His words stirred anxieties she was trying for the moment not to think about and, sticking her chin out defiantly, she murmured, 'I'll cope.'

'Yes,' he accepted on a harshly released breath. 'That's what I'm afraid of.' There was hard disparagement in the deep voice, in the tough rigidity of his jaw. 'In an expensive flat? With no transport? And what will you do when you're out temping? Employ a nanny? You'll be lucky even to be able to pay her bus-fare on a secretary's pay! Or was that taken into consideration out of the money you squeezed out of me to father your child?'

Recoiling from his understandable accusation, she searched for some satisfactory answer. But only honesty could redeem her, she realised hopelessly, remaining silent as relentlessly he went on.

'You're going to wind up in a crummy little bed-sit—living off the state, Nadine. And I'll be darned if I'll allow any offspring of mine to endure an existence like I had. Shunted around from aunt to aunt while its mother's off somewhere trying to earn a living. Living hand to mouth, trying to make ends meet. Wearing the stigma not only of illegitimacy but of deprivation...' He laughed coarsely at the shock that had manifested itself on Nadine's face. 'Oh, yes. Didn't you know?'

No, she hadn't, she thought, stunned, unable wholly to believe it. The inimitable Cameron Hunter? Illegitimate? Poor?

'So you didn't.'

Her face must have told him that, she realised, while her brain was still deducing what mental strength and character must have brought him from such humble beginnings to occupy the respected position he held today. The knowledge only served to make her feel even more intimidated by him.

'No, Lisa didn't tell me,' she said quietly.

'I wonder why?'

Had she imagined that sudden drag of breath through his lungs, that sharpened edge to his voice? Or was she mistaking deep, masculine pain...?

'Has she...? I mean, have you heard anything——?' She broke off, hesitating, flinching as he came back with a swift, cutting retort.

'Do you really care?' Tension made the line of his cheek more prominent, whether from anger or some other personal emotion Nadine wasn't sure. 'Well, you're going to be made to care—for the future of our child if nothing else,' he promised with inexorable softness. 'And just in case you've got any ideas of flitting off somewhere where you think I can't reach you, you're going to pack in both that job and that flat of yours and live under my roof—in my cottage—as originally arranged, until the child's born!'

A surge of hot anger burned through Nadine's veins from his supreme arrogance. 'That's what you think!'

she riposted determinedly. There was no way she was agreeing to that! He was right, though. She wanted to get as far away from him as she possibly could, to minimise the risk of his trying to take the baby away from her. 'You can hardly force me to, can you?' she challenged him on a small note of defiance.

And perhaps he realised it too, she thought, relieved when his mouth firmed in what she could only deduce was frustrated acknowledgment and he went on to ask in an almost bored tone, 'How's your mother keeping these days?'

Glancing out at the eternal queues at the bus-stops, the endless traffic, Nadine felt her body stiffen. 'All right.' It was difficult to lie—to pretend.

'What did she say when you told her you were pregnant?'

She looked at him quickly. Why did he want to know that?

Unconsciously her fingers tightened around the handbag on her lap. 'I haven't,' she answered, as non-chalantly as she was able.

'Oh?' Cursorily he glanced across at her, his gaze travelling down over the shallow rising of her breasts to her fingers curling tensely into the soft fabric of her bag. 'But you're going to? Or are you planning not to chance a visit home until after you've given birth?'

He sounded mildly amused and she said, 'Of course I'll tell her.'

'But you won't be telling her the absolute truth?'

She made a distinct effort to relax as she saw his glance stray casually to her hands again. 'No,' she responded cautiously, wondering why he had sounded so sure.

'What are you going to tell her?'

'I don't know,' she murmured, and was glad when he leaned across to close the central air-vents, because the exhaust fumes from a dusty van in front were making her feel sick.

He started talking casually about pollution then, and the growing congestion in the city—things she felt strongly enough about herself to be able to engage in sympathetic discussion with him until he turned into the street of smart, semi-detached houses, pulling up outside her flat.

'There you are,' he said almost congenially, a smile touching his lips as he clicked the handbrake into place, and then, surprisingly, pulled the keys out of the ignition. 'Now, do as you're told and go up and pack as many things as you'll need to see you through a long stay in the country, because you're moving into that cottage tonight!'

Startled flecks showed in Nadine's green eyes as she stared at him. 'By whose authority?' she snapped, flabbergasted.

'By your own glimmer of a conscience, Nadine.' Leather squeaked softly as he turned to face her, one finely clad arm resting disturbingly across the back of her seat. 'Unless, of course, you would prefer me to pen a very detailed and informative account of your behaviour to your mother—?'

'You wouldn't dare!'

He didn't even need to answer that. Seeing the inexorable determination on that uncompromising mouth, Nadine realised now what he had been doing when he had asked those seemingly casual questions about her mother. He'd been testing the water, as the saying went— or her reaction anyway—understanding her body language with all the skill and shrewdness of his profession.

He'd obviously heard her telling Lisa all those weeks before not to mention their arrangement to Dawn Kendall if she, Nadine, did become pregnant; had heard her begging Lisa, making her promise. He'd clearly realised how desperate she'd been to keep it from her mother, even if he hadn't known—still didn't know—the reason why. And now she'd played right into his hands! she thought hopelessly, without seeing the manipulation behind those cleverly posed questions. Otherwise she could have said she'd already told her mother the truth, or that she was intending to. Anything but suffer this humiliating defeat.

'You calculating bastard.'

'Right on target.' He smiled without warmth, bringing embarrassed colour to her cheeks as she realised the hard-hitting implication of what she had just called him. 'And as far as the adjective goes, that makes two of us, doesn't it?' he said smoothly, aware of her embarrassment as he got out and came round to open her door with a courtesy that surprised her in the circumstances.

It only took an hour for her to pack the things she needed to take, although she filled a large suitcase and a substantial-sized travelling bag.

'Leave that,' Cameron ordered when she went to pick it up to follow him down with her suitcase to the car.

'Why? Scared I might overdo things?' she couldn't help taunting sarcastically, but he ignored it, stooping to pick up the travelling bag with her case and carrying them both effortlessly downstairs.

She had been in the bathroom, checking that she hadn't forgotten anything, and heard Cameron coming back just as she came out into the hall.

'Let's get one thing straight,' he advised grimly, 'before we go any further, and that's that I don't care an iota what happens to you. But I am concerned for the welfare of my child, and while you're carrying it you'll take every possible precaution to protect it. Do I make myself clear?'

Perfectly, she thought, trying to deny just how much his confessed lack of concern for her had hurt. And, of course, she was going to take every step necessary to safeguard her baby. But she didn't tell him that, snapping back instead, 'What will you do? Pass sentence on me if I don't?' And with that deliberately provocative remark she brushed past him with her chin in the air, out to the gleaming saloon.

It was dark when they arrived at the cottage—Cameron's insistence on stopping for a meal en route, which she had felt too nauseous to eat, which he had interpreted as rebellion, having necessitated a good hour's break in their journey.

Now, as they pulled up in the country lane outside the solitary little house, Nadine's stomach seemed to come up into her mouth.

'Would you give me a minute?' she uttered as he started getting out of the car, despising herself for the way it had come out—as an almost feeble appeal. She didn't want to make a fuss—show any weakness in front of him.

'What's wrong?'

'I feel sick.' Suddenly she was forced to swallow her pride and tell him, leaning sharply forward, her hand clamped over her mouth.

'I thought that was a morning problem,' he remarked when she sat back again.

'So did I.' Feeling easier, she uttered an ironic little laugh. 'I think my body-clock's stuck permanently on a.m. at the moment.'

'Why the hell didn't you tell me?' He sounded surprisingly concerned, but she merely shrugged, deciding against reminding him of his earlier remark about not caring about her. 'You've been to sleep,' he said laconically—which was something, she thought, that she seemed to be doing all the time lately. 'That might not have helped. Wait here.'

He got out of the car and she watched his tall, shadowy figure moving through the little gate, along the garden path; she heard the jangle of keys then the door opening, before light flooded through the aperture, spilling out across the step and two superb hydrangea bushes that were growing near the house.

'Come on.' The touch of his hand on her elbow was gentle if not caring, and unwelcome sensations assailed her as she teetered unsteadily and felt a supportive arm go across her back.

'I'm all right,' she protested with mild vehemence, trying to pull away.

'The devil you are.' He swore roughly under his breath. 'And it isn't going to help not eating properly. You're going to get something inside you,' he asserted, that strong arm keeping her locked to his side as he guided her along the path.

'I couldn't,' she uttered, her mind rejecting his electrifying nearness as much as her stomach rejected the thought of food.

'You can and you will. You'll eat little and often and drink plenty of fluids,' he told her, surprising her with a knowledge of her condition she hadn't expected him to possess. 'You might think you can't stomach anything, but it will help the nausea, believe me.'

On that, at least, she thought later, when she was sitting on the floral-patterned settee tucking into the dry toast and tea he had made her, he had been right, because the sickness had certainly begun to subside.

'Did...you and Lisa come here for weekends?' she asked hesitantly as he came in from the car with her luggage. The room, though spacious and well-furnished, reflected an old-world charm which was certainly not Lisa's taste, she thought, remembering her friend's liking for stark, contemporary designs.

'No,' he answered, and so tersely that she wondered if she should have mentioned it since he was still obviously blaming her for the break-up of his marriage. But then, in surprisingly neutral tones, he said, 'Lisa never stayed here. This place belonged to an aunt of mine, and when she died last year it passed to me. I don't get down here as often as I'd like, but it's always been the perfect spot to come when I want to unwind and get life back into perspective. It's also where I did a lot of my growing up.'

Of course. He had said he'd lived with various aunts, Nadine remembered, feeling the sudden throb of her pulse as her gaze clashed with his, the dark sapphire of his eyes holding hers with a hard, unsettling intensity.

What was he thinking? she wondered, weakened by a sexual magnetism she didn't want to acknowledge. Because he had discarded his tie, loosened the pristine white shirt, so that she was disturbed by mental images of the last time she had seen him like that, in that other country house, but determinedly she pushed them out of her mind.

He might appeal to every feminine instinct she possessed, but she was only here with him now because of the consequences of that other time; because she was expecting his baby—the baby he had planned to share with Lisa. But he *was* still Lisa's husband, and it was only because it was *his* baby that he was showing any concern or responsibility towards her, Nadine. What secret feelings she might harbour for him counted for nothing.

'You look tired.' Cameron's voice was coolly detached. 'I think you'd better go to bed. Come on, I'll show you your room.'

His tone stirred a reckless rebellion in her, but she didn't have the energy to argue and compliantly she went ahead of him, up the creaking stairs.

The room he showed her into had the same quaint charm as the sitting-room: the coverlet on the double bed matching the gaily floral curtains and valance, the predominant leafy greens picking out the natural green in the carpet.

'The bathroom's next door,' he informed her, lifting her case up on to the chest beside the door. 'If you need anything just call. I'm just along the corridor.'

Picking up on his last words, Nadine looked at him quickly. 'Aren't you . . . going back tonight?' she asked, realising how foolish that sounded in view of the hour, and despairing of herself for letting him see how unsettled that made her feel as he smiled, mockingly aware.

'No, Nadine, I'm not.' He strode across to the bed where he deposited her travelling bag. 'Were you imagining I was? Would you feel happier if the father of your child wasn't around? Is that it?'

When she didn't answer, too weary to launch herself into another verbal battle with him, he said, 'Well, I'm going to be around—at every available opportunity. No child of mine is going to be deprived of its father— whether its mother likes it or not! So you'd better get used to the idea, sweetheart, and you'd better get used to it now!'

As he'd spoken he had tugged back the bedcovers on one side to reveal the crisp white pillowcases. Signs of a woman's touch, Nadine couldn't help thinking, although he had said Lisa didn't come to the cottage. She guessed that he had someone in on a regular basis to clean.

'You didn't have to drag me away from my job—not so soon, anyway,' Nadine protested tiredly, although feeling as she did at the moment she wasn't totally averse to a break. 'What am I supposed to do for the next few months, buried down here, miles from anywhere?'

'I'm sure you'll think of something,' he drawled, pulling the chintzy curtains on the night-shrouded countryside. 'And, as I said, I'll make it my business to be around as often as I can. It might not be what you want, but you were certainly quick enough to agree to it when you were planning this little campaign of single motherhood for yourself. What you seemed to overlook was that it takes two to accomplish conception, and in any form of partnership you can't have all your own way. When you're over the worst and feeling better you can get back to your typewriter, if you feel inclined to, but I don't see any point in your wasting all your valuable legal experience in some insurance office. You'll probably find more job satisfaction—and certainly less risk to our child—working here, for me.'

Feeling the dressing-table immediately behind her, Nadine leaned back, with her hands on its smooth surface to steady herself, rocked by the absolute audacity of the man.

'Why?' she enquired brittly, too bruised and angered by his mistaken opinion of her even to try to defend herself, or to wonder exactly what he was proposing. 'As surety? To make sure I pay back all the money you think I wheedled out of you?' She finished with bitter cynicism, because—heaven help her!—she would. She didn't know how. But somehow—some day—she would!

She caught her breath as he came too close for her to move away from the dressing-table, that elusive scent of him playing dangerous games with her senses as he caught her small chin between his thumb and forefinger and said, 'Oh, you'll pay.' His tone was lethally soft. 'But not in the way you're imagining, Nadine. Money doesn't even figure in the cost you're going to have to settle with me. Now go to bed, like a good girl. Unless of course...' His gaze strayed down across the inviting softness of the bed so that, panicking, she pushed at him with all her strength and caught his softly mocking laughter as he went out.

CHAPTER THREE

WHEN Nadine awoke the sun was shining through a chink in the heavy floral curtains and, curious to see exactly where she was, she clambered out of bed.

The room obviously faced east, she realised as she pulled back the curtains, squinting from the dazzling rays of the sun. It was reflected almost blindingly by the gleaming bodywork of the Mercedes, which was parked beneath her window in the lane. On the other side, beyond a five-bar gate, fields stretched away to forestry and gently rolling hills, while in the immediate meadow—partly flanked on the lane-side by a row of chestnut trees—two horses grazed, coats brown and sleek, at one with the still, peaceful morning. No wonder Cameron had said it was a good place to unwind!

A tap on her door made her turn sharply, suddenly conscious of her short white lacy nightie. And she must have hesitated too long with her quiet, tentative, 'Yes,' or might simply not have been heard, because suddenly Cameron was coming in, although he stopped instantly when he saw her.

'I thought you'd still be in bed,' he remarked, obviously surprised. His glance over the feminine nightdress that she knew revealed far too much of her legs lifted to the tousled riot of auburn hair. 'I didn't bring you a tray as I wasn't sure how much you could stomach in the mornings, but if you feel like something more than just dry toast it's all prepared.'

This caring, domesticated side of him was so different from the hard antagonist who had left her the previous night that the disparity threw her for a moment. That, and the fact that the light cotton T-shirt he was wearing with pale, well-tailored trousers showed the muscular strength of his chest and broad shoulders, emphasising the hard, lean line of his waist.

'No. J-just toast,' she stammered, although remarkably she didn't feel too bad this morning, she realised, as quickly she tagged on, 'And it's all right. I'll be down.'

'Why? Does my being in your room make you feel uncomfortable?' he quizzed, with that sensual mouth curving sardonically. Hitting the nail on the head! she thought as he turned and went out before she could even think of a suitable response.

He didn't appear to be around when she came down into the sunny breakfast-room, although the round oak table was laid for two, with the second place having already been cleared. The smell of freshly toasted bread hung appetisingly on the air. She could see three slices in the toast-rack. And there was a freshly made pot of tea steaming under a padded cosy, even though she could still smell the lingering and rather nauseating aroma of coffee he had obviously made for himself. Clearly he'd remembered her saying yesterday how her pregnancy had given her an aversion to it, she thought, with a reluctant gratitude to him for that much at least.

He didn't reappear before she had eaten two slices of the toast with honey and almost drained the teapot, and, having finished, she got up from the table, tugging at the rather tight waistband of her jeans. Soon she would have to leave them off for something a little more comfortable, she realised with a grimace, but at that moment there was something more pressing on her mind. Something she should have done last night, if she hadn't been so exhausted, and which she could do more easily now while Cameron wasn't around.

Crossing the little passage to the sitting-room and the phone that stood on the table behind the door, feeling like a criminal, afraid of being caught, quickly she dialled the number of the convalescent home.

'Hello. It's me, Nadine.'

The sister, a bright, breezy woman, informed her that Dawn Kendall was out, undergoing a routine appointment at the hospital, and instantly launched into a comforting patter on how the rehabilitation exercises were helping her immensely, telling Nadine that she shouldn't worry.

'Thanks. You don't know what that means to me.' She smiled, visibly relaxing, and then, hearing a sound along the passage, said quickly, much more quietly, 'I've moved out of the flat, but you can reach me at this number——' hurriedly she conveyed it to the sister '—if you need to call me at all.'

She tried to put the phone down quietly, and only succeeded in dropping it into its cradle with a noisy little clatter, realising how guilty she must have appeared as, with a little gasp, she whirled round to see Cameron watching her from the doorway.

'Well, well. Have I caught you ringing someone you'd rather I didn't know about?' His smile was purely superficial as he strode in with a predator's watchfulness behind that casually relaxed poise. 'I wonder why?'

Swallowing, she wanted to tell him. To cry out how seriously ill her mother had been, that she'd agreed to have this baby to help her. But she was afraid that if she did he might use the knowledge as an even more effective weapon against her. And then there was the promise she'd made to her mother, so that anger and frustration had her hurling back instead, 'You can wonder all you like! I do happen to have a private life, you know!'

'Not while you're here—and not while you're pregnant with my child, you don't! Not as far as other men are concerned anyway!'

So that was what he thought!

'And what makes you think it was——?' Cheeks flaming, Nadine desisted from adding 'another man', knowing that at any minute she'd be in danger of blurting out the truth. 'I'm not your wife, Cameron,' she stressed with cutting emphasis, the declaration stabbing at her own heart. 'And if I want to see anyone else I will, and I'd like to see you stop me!'

The tangible anger in his eyes told her she'd been a perfect fool in challenging him like that, because suddenly he was moving towards her, intimidation in every lithe inch of him as he breathed with a frightening calmness, 'Would you?'

Unnerved by the daunting purpose behind that cool veneer, Nadine took a few steps back. Why couldn't she have kept her mouth shut? 'For heaven's sake, Cameron, all we made was a contract...'

'Yes, and one you reneged on,' he reminded her with a flaying softness. 'Oh, no you don't!' With reflexes sharp as a jungle cat's, he'd put down the carton of milk he'd obviously gone out for and was hauling her against him, preventing her swift attempt to dart away. 'You want it all, don't you?'

Fearfully she shot her hands up to push futilely against the smooth cotton of his shirt. She could feel the bulge of muscle, the beating strength of his anger beneath. 'Cameron, please...'

He laughed softly and humourlessly, that derisive gaze raking over the shining fire of her hair, her anger-flushed features, the panic-filled look in her green eyes. 'Oh, yes, we've been there before, haven't we?' he breathed tauntingly, and with mortifying clarity she realised that he was referring to her abandoned response to him in the privacy of that hotel room when, aroused to fever-pitch, she'd sobbed out her involuntary pleas.

'You bastard!' Her flush deepened to crimson. She wanted to forget that weekend, and pushed at him with all the force of her humiliation, but it was no use. His strength was impregnable, and her breath left her in a gush as the iron bar of his arm pulled her closer to him, to the antagonised length of his firm, threatening masculinity.

'What's wrong, Nadine? Ashamed to admit that I actually had you begging——?'

'Stop it!'

His smile was cruel. 'Why? Don't you like remembering how you responded to me?' Contemptuously his gaze touched on the soft perfection of her mouth, the pale skin above the open 'V' of her blouse. 'As you'd respond to me again if I touched you.'

Panic leaped through her as rebellion vied with a reckless excitement in her blood, making her writhe in his merciless grasp. 'You conceited...!'

He laughed at her vain efforts to free herself. 'Perhaps, but I prefer to call it mutual attraction,' he expressed, punctuating those last words with harsh emphasis as the fingers of his free hand twisted in her hair, dragging her head back to expose the smooth line of her throat.

'No, Cameron, please...'

She closed her eyes against the mocking cruelty of his, aware only of the thunder of his heart beneath her hands as she waited for his humiliating assault. It was, therefore, a shock to her when his lips burned gently across her sensitive flesh to the pulse beating frantically in the hollow of her throat and he whispered, in a voice as soft as his action, 'That isn't what you were saying last time.'

Burning with shame, she twisted angrily in his grasp, which only incensed him to tighten his hold on her. His dark hair was touching her cheek; she could smell the clean, fresh smell of the shampoo he had used, sensations shivering traitorously through her from the intimate contact of his body, from the increasingly sensual torture of his lips against her skin.

'You never begged any other man, did you?' His voice was hoarse with the intensity of his loathing, and with something else—something that shuddered through him and which she recognised as the raw edge of desire. 'If you had, no other man would have been strong enough to hold out against that treacherous sorcery...'

The hand in her hair had moved to cradle her head, and she uttered a small, strangled sound as his mouth came down hard over hers, his other arm locking her to him with relentless tenacity.

Excitement raced through her as his mouth plundered hers, demanding the subjugation of her rapidly diminishing will, and she didn't know at what point he moved slightly, so that her hands could slide up to his shoulders, knew only that every instinct of rebellion was being crushed and was glorying in its own defeat by the hard invasion of his mouth, by the bitter-sweet memory of the pleasure those lips and hands had given her, a pleasure she wanted—needed . . .!

'Damn you to hell, Nadine!' She gave a small, frustrated cry as he broke abruptly away from her. 'What are you driving me to?' he snarled breathlessly, the tremor in his voice revealing just how out of control he was, and that he was angry with himself because of it, his chest lifting heavily beneath the soft shirt. 'While you're living in my house, you'll do so under *my* terms, is that clear?'

Too shaken to respond, Nadine turned away to stare blindly out of the window, hearing Cameron storm angrily out of the room.

She felt like running after him, flinging the truth at him about Lisa and the other man, vindicating herself by letting him know just what her real reason was for wanting to keep her baby, but integrity and common sense prevailed. If there was a chance that he and Lisa might get back together . . .

The thought induced an involuntary closing of her eyes, her breath shuddering through her lungs. Any revelation about her friend . . . Correction. Ex-friend, she amended mentally, with the sudden burn of tears against her lids. Any revelation could severely hamper that chance, and she couldn't be a party to that any more than she could tell him the truth about that phone call, which was the only way she could have made him realise that she wasn't the calculating creature he believed her to be. Dear heaven! What a mess! she thought wretchedly.

Reluctant to face him again so soon after her humiliating response to him, she went back up to her room, to unpack the suitcase she had been too tired to empty the previous night.

He was right, she thought, despairing of herself. He had only to touch her...

Hanging a blouse in the old mahogany wardrobe, she tried to shake all thoughts of that kiss and her response to it out of her mind. The man despised her, she reminded herself. If he didn't—hadn't wanted to punish her for all he believed her guilty of—he wouldn't even have come near her, she thought with a little pierce of anguish inside.

Consequently, after writing a notelet to her mother in which she skimmed over the details of her change of job and her subsequent move to the country, she was surprised when, coming downstairs with the intention of popping out to post it, she met Cameron coming up and he said casually, 'I'm driving over to Bath this afternoon. Would you care to come?'

She wished she had the strength of will to resist his invitation, but there were a few things she wanted to buy in town. Besides, she had never seen Bath—other than the glimpse she had had of its outskirts after they had left the motorway the previous night—and before she realised it she was responding, 'Thanks, I'd like to.'

And that was how, after a light lunch, prepared between them with surprisingly little animosity, she found herself sitting in the powerful saloon, actually looking forward to the afternoon.

'You said something last night about me working for you.' Tentatively she raised the subject as they were travelling through a village that gave on to a view of rolling Somerset hills. She felt awkward, recalling the circumstances which had led him to suggest it, but curious because he hadn't said anything about it since.

'Yes.' Silently he brought the car to halt at the junction of the country road before proceeding on to a roundabout. 'I thought you might appreciate some typing to do over the next few weeks, in which case there will be a whole book to bash out if you feel like keeping busy.'

'A book?' Pushing her differences with him to the back of her mind, Nadine looked at him interestedly. 'One you've written?' she enquired, with a light lift of finely arched brows.

'Oh, nothing that's going to carry you off into the wonderful realms of fantasy or me into the bestseller stakes.' His laughter mocked any suggestion of his ability to involve himself in fiction. 'It's a technical book, I'm afraid—regarding the reformation of certain aspects of the law.'

'Oh?' Fascinated, Nadine suddenly felt herself relaxing with him. 'You think the law needs reforming? I thought you were content to administer it as it was.'

He slanted her a wry glance as he put his foot down to take a stretch of dual carriageway, obviously detecting that censorious little note in her voice. 'Just because I represent it, it doesn't mean I have to be satisfied with it,' he expressed with a surprising depth of emotion.

Knowing him from past experience, she thought, No, you expect perfection, and when you don't get it you're as frustrated as hell.

'So what changes would you like to see?' she prompted, and he answered without hesitation.

'The tightening of far too many loopholes.' He gave her some examples and then said, 'More powers for judges as regards sentencing. A more acceptable means of funding the legal aid system, plus a fairer chance at justice for the poor.'

His concern for the underprivileged surprised her until she remembered what he had revealed about himself while they were still in London yesterday. Of course he'd care—and deeply. His concern for her while she was pregnant, and for the welfare of the baby she was carrying, should have assured her of that.

'But doesn't it disturb you sometimes, defending someone—trying to prove that person's innocence—when you know inside, deep down, that they're probably guilty? How do you justify a thing like that?'

'It isn't a case of trying to prove a guilty man innocent,' he said, his lips curving slightly at the frankness of her question. 'It's simply to disclaim any proof of that guilt beyond all reasonable doubt. There's a difference.'

It was an interesting definition, and one which put like that she could easily appreciate—along with the sheer skill, discipline and hard-headed insight it must have taken to make him a master of his profession.

'Could that be why so many innocent people are wrongly convicted?' Nadine challenged, reeling off several such cases that had sprung instantly to mind, and inducing a subtle lift of a thick, masculine brow that told her he was impressed. An absurd pleasure stole through her blood. 'It makes one ask if a return to the old medieval system might not be just as reliable, doesn't it?' she uttered, pulling a wry face.

He laughed, showing perfect white teeth. 'What are you advocating? Trial by ordeal? Throwing them in the river——' his smile was almost breath-catching '—and if they float they're guilty?'

'And if they drown they're innocent,' Nadine supplied drily, thinking, Perhaps that's what you should do to me? Maybe then I'd stand a better chance of proving you're wrong about me. Trying, though, to convince herself that it didn't matter one way or the other what he thought, she added more sombrely, 'Is it any less civilised than relying on one's particular counsel to give the best performance on the day?'

Cameron's mouth firmed as he steered the car along beside the ancient high wall flanking the beautiful Georgian city, those long, dark hands strong and competent on the wheel. Hands in which, often, people placed the very fabric of their existence, she thought with a little shiver of unwilling admiration for him. And she knew in that moment that if something happened where she had legally to prove her own innocence, then, despite everything he believed about her, she wouldn't want to place herself in anyone else's hands but his.

'Somehow I like to think the job I do is something more beneficial than just acting out a role,' he told her with a grimace. And then, as the road opened up over the river, with the vast arches of the railway bridge towering above them on the right, he said smugly, 'Here you are,' obviously remembering her saying that she'd never seen Avon's spa city before. 'This is Bath.'

Fortressed by hills, the terraces and elegant crescents of the city rose with the surrounding terrain, the warm tones of the Georgian buildings—constructed of local stone—lending a sympathetic blend of dignity and grace to the natural ambience.

Cameron parked the car in a multi-storey car park near the station and then proceeded to show her one or two famous features of the city like the ancient baths—built by the Romans to utilise the mineral springs that had made Bath such a fashionable health resort in the eighteenth century—and the dominating structure of the abbey where, as Cameron pointed out to her, Edgar, the first King of England was crowned in 973.

Over a thousand years ago, Nadine calculated. She thought, as they left the abbey precincts for the newer part of town, of the changes the city had seen over that vast span of years—architecturally, at least, from its quaint, medieval alleys and the grand Palladian style of the Georgians to the modern-day centre with its wonderful shops, which included a particularly delightful stationer's where Cameron bought some materials for the book he was writing.

'I'll get hold of a word-processor for you if it'll make your life easier,' he offered as they came out of the shop. 'I don't type, so it would have been no use to me. I've written the whole thing in longhand, and as you'll probably remember, from having suffered working with me before, my writing's hardly the most legible at the best of times.'

As if she could forget! 'That's all right. I'll just ring you up every time I get stuck,' she threatened, looking up at him with a facetious glitter in her eyes. The earlier tension between them had dissolved during the journey, and she was enjoying looking around the city; she was enjoying Cameron's company too, although she refused to allow herself to dwell too much on that.

'Look where you're going!' he advised with a hint of laughter in his voice. The touch of his hands on her shoulders as he prevented her from colliding with a woman who was passing with a pushchair was casually impersonal, yet enough to cause her heart to leap in her breast.

'I took my degree here in Bath,' he mentioned to her later as they strolled over a bridge graced by black wrought-iron lamps, spaced at intervals with ornate stone bowls along the wall. 'Very frugal days, when we seemed to exist at starvation level, doing any odd job at weekends to get some extra cash, and when the sun shone swotting like devils——' this with a jerk of his chin '—down there in that park.'

Keen to know all she could about him, she glanced over the wall to where the river cascaded in a tumble of frothy white foam down over the bow-shaped terraces of the weir. A little way ahead was the park he had indicated, vibrant with flowers, where a brass band played, unobserved today by the students who now, at the height of summer, would have left the city for the long holiday—as the young Cameron Hunter once had. Now, though, because of all his hard work and determination, he could put the years of poverty behind him, bask in the comfort of a luxury home, a coveted life-style, in the satisfaction of the most respected of professions.

'What are you thinking?'

Nadine dragged her gaze from the tumbling water to catch the deep blue eyes watching her intently.

'About the advantages of education,' she parried with a nervous little laugh. But in a way, she thought, it was true.

'You weren't at university?'

It was something he already knew. But she answered. 'No. For that I'd have had to have stayed on at school, and I didn't.' And that had been because her father had walked out when she'd been barely in her early teens and her mother had needed all the financial help she could get, she appended silently as she watched a gull soaring over the river, although she didn't tell Cameron that.

'Pity,' he said, and that was all.

And seeing the dark concentration on that strong profile as he gazed back towards the pigeon-clothed Georgian buildings spanning the bridge, she wondered what *he* was thinking. That no offspring of his would be allowed to jeopardise its opportunity to have the best possible chance in life? A little twist of apprehension spiralled through her as she acknowledged the sort of man he was. Intuitively she knew he had made no idle threat when he had said that where any child of his was concerned he would always be involved.

'Are you hungry?' he asked her then, and when she realised she was he took her to a quaint little tea-shop with panelled walls and exposed beams, which turned out to be the oldest house in Bath, where she drank three cups of tea while tucking into the biggest tea-cake she had ever eaten.

'I'll be putting on weight fast enough without this!' she laughed, as she cut through the soft, light dough. Called a Sally Lunn, the cake was a specialty of the house, and she'd ordered hers with cinnamon butter, which came melted over the bun like a hot and spicy, chocolate-brown sauce and tasted as delicious as it smelt.

'You're beginning to sound like Lisa.'

Nadine looked up quickly.

If it hurt to talk about his wife then he was certainly concealing it well, because no emotion flawed the striking framework of his features, and his tone, when he'd spoken, had been almost casual.

'Am I?' she asked, glancing out at a man walking a small dog in the narrow street beyond the shop's bow window, feeling more awkward about discussing her old friend than Cameron obviously appeared to be.

Some deep, personal feeling hardened the strong lines of his face and he said rather harshly, 'Are you worried about motherhood ruining that beautiful figure?'

As Lisa had been? With a rush of conflicting emotions arising from both his disparaging tone and his rather back-handed compliment, she drew her attention from a splendid Hanoverian arch dividing the two sections of the tea-room to answer somewhat tartly, 'No, I'm not! I happen to think a baby's more important than a few stretch-marks and a sagging bustline!' So stick that in your pipe and smoke it! she thought waspishly, stabbing her fork into the last portion of her bun with a single-mindedness that said she wished it was him.

'Want another?' was all he responded drily, as he watched her scooping up the remaining dark butter sauce. Which preposterous suggestion induced her, as he had intended it should, to smile.

'You must be joking!' she breathed, popping that last piece into her mouth and clutching her stomach.

'Well...' He shrugged, that meaningful syllable with that knowing quirk of the lips conveying that he wasn't oblivious to the curious fancies of women in her condition. Oddly embarrassed, she glanced away, down at that strong, tapered hand reaching for the bill the waitress had left.

Strangely, he wasn't wearing his wedding-ring. The absence of the thick gold band she had been used to seeing on his finger jolted her for a moment, bringing myriad questions leaping into her brain.

Had he simply forgotten to put it on? Or was its removal a conscious acceptance of his marriage being over? Was he hurting inside? Aching for the woman he loved—the woman he had planned to build a life with? Or had he resigned himself to the fact that Lisa wasn't ever coming back?

She looked up and realised that he had caught her watching him, seen where her interest lay, and she blushed, conscious of the colour staining her cheeks. She could see the brilliant glitter of some inimical emotion in those blue eyes, and wondered if it sprang from a bitter anger towards Lisa or, more probably, hatred for *her*, and she half expected him to make some cutting comment about her being responsible, but he merely enquired, 'Ready?' And when she nodded, he rose, barely giving her time to drain her cup before rasping, 'Then let's get out and get some air.'

The rest of the day passed with a return of its earlier tension, though, amazingly, Cameron decided to spend the following day at the cottage, too.

While he was busy doing some work in one of the upstairs rooms, Nadine sat outside under the shade of a gnarled plum tree in the rear garden, looking up occasionally from browsing through his unfinished manuscript to watch a bright butterfly flitting over the white and yellow alyssum bordering the path, or a bird dart out of the orchard beyond and skim away, low across the adjacent fields.

Cameron had certainly been right, though, she thought, grimacing, as she returned to reading his book. His writing hadn't improved with the years! It was the hand of a man too busy with important issues to worry about anything so trivial as legibility, yet it was bold and flowing, his character stamped on every hastily scrawled word. Still, she had all week to work it out, she reflected thankfully, because that was when he said he'd be coming back with the word-processor. Craving for a cup of tea, she left his manuscript under a small stone on her chair, to secure it from a playful breeze, and went inside to put the kettle on and look for Cameron.

He wasn't in any of the upstairs rooms, but, hearing noises overhead, she came across a portable ladder that had been pulled down some way along an upper landing, which led through a trap door into the loft.

'What are you doing?'

Seeing Cameron, head bowed in concentration, sorting through a trunk, she thought she might at least have startled him as she poked her head through the hatch.

But his nerves were steel-bound, she decided, because he didn't even flinch, glancing up with only a modicum of surprise to see her there before answering, 'This place needs insulating, but before that can be done the whole loft needs clearing out. And what the devil do you think you're doing, climbing ladders in your condition?'

'I'm hardly infirm, am I?' she responded dismissively, stepping up into the attic, inhaling the scent of ancient dust as she looked delightedly around. It was a storeroom of abandoned history: old pictures, plates with their glaze cracked and grimy, long-discarded furniture and, near a wall, where the roof-line sloped steeply, a rocking-horse with a matted white mane and tail, its flaking dappled paint a silent statement of years of pleasurable use.

'Was this yours?'

She was already on the wooden planking which was serving as a temporary floor, moving eagerly across to the horse, when she heard Cameron shout from behind, 'Watch where you're going, for goodness sake!'

Nadine gasped at the arm that was suddenly locking hard around her middle, preventing her from moving any further. 'These boards don't go right over there— those joists are all exposed. Put a foot between those and you're likely to wind up in the bathroom sink,' he admonished. 'Followed probably by a spell in bed with a miscarriage.'

His tone implied that he still thought she had no business coming up there in the first place, yet his concern prompted her, unthinkingly, to say, 'I would have thought you would have considered that an end to a lot of problems,' and she felt the muscles of his body behind her lock tight, heard the hiss of his breath through his lungs.

'Just promise me here and now that you'll never let that idea cross that devious little mind of yours again,' he rasped, the breath he released a hot intimation against her cheek.

'No,' she said shakily by way of affirmation, frightened by that latent anger in him, by the riveting awareness of that arm still lying across her middle, of the hand resting casually on her hip.

And, as though he had suddenly become aware of it too, abruptly he released her, saying tightly, 'Stay on the boards. And, no, the horse belonged to my grandmother and then my aunt—not to me.'

'It's as old as that!' Nadine looked appreciatively towards the magnificent toy, something which, as a child, she had always wanted but, because of her father's inability to keep a steady job and his love of high living, she thought, feeling only sadness for him now, she had never had. 'But she let you ride it?' she added as a foregone conclusion, knowing a strange surge of emotion in picturing him as a small boy, and then older, cycling on the rusting bike she had caught sight of propped up in a corner, around the Somerset lanes.

'Yes, she let me ride it. Now, what are you doing up here?'

There was a hint of impatience in his voice and Nadine wondered why. Didn't he want her up here for some reason—other than the risk he thought she was taking for herself and the baby?

'I was going to make a cup of tea. I came up to ask if you—— Gosh! What's that?'

He was lifting an old shoe-box out of the trunk. The lid was broken on one side and several photographs fell out, and Nadine stooped to pick them up. One or two of them were in sepia, edges broken and curling with age, and there were several more recent ones too—snapshots in black and white.

'Who's this?' she enquired, holding up one of a laughing young woman, barely out of her teens, who looked as if she was laughing at life, without a care in the world.

Cameron sent a cursory glance towards it and carried on taking things out of the trunk. 'That's my mother,' he stated tonelessly.

Surprised, Nadine stared at the photograph, recognising the wilful determination behind the laughter, and the arresting symmetry of the features, both of which she had passed on to her son. A faint scent impinged on her nostrils, a smell of damp soot from a crack in the old chimney.

'She's beautiful,' she uttered quietly.

'Yes, she is.' His voice was low and clipped.

'How old was she then?' Nadine asked, sensing that he didn't particularly want to talk about it. But the desire to discover all she could about this private and very complex man, by whom she'd been enthralled for what seemed like forever, fed her curiosity.

'Nineteen. It was taken the year before she had me.'

And then everything changed. He didn't say it, but she could tell from that censuring note in his voice that he considered himself instrumental in causing the woman's unhappiness. Taking a deep breath, she said quickly, 'It was her choice.' And then, swiftly, 'Wasn't it?' she added, alarm creasing the smooth contours of her face as she suddenly wondered if perhaps she'd been too hasty in her assumption, if the woman might have been the victim of some dreadful assault.

'What do you know about it?' he rasped, his eyes suddenly storm-dark and accusing. 'She was young and foolishly in love—unable to see beyond the ecstasy of sublime passion. She was never like that——' that strong chin jerked towards the photograph '—as I remember her. She was thin and drawn and always dressed in cast-offs, worn out with working and trying to provide for herself as well as a kid.'

'And your father?' Pushing her shining hair back off her face, she asked the question gingerly. 'Did you know him?' It was something she'd been wondering ever since he'd revealed the details of his childhood to her in the car the other day.

At this he abandoned whatever he'd been taking out of the trunk, standing with hands splayed firmly against the narrow angles of his hips.

'What is this? Twenty questions?' he demanded, his face taut with formidable anger, the casually buttoned denim pulling tightly across his chest, revealing the dark velvet of his skin and the coarse, curling black hair that stated the hard, exciting virility of his body. 'If it keeps you quiet, no, I didn't know him. I knew nothing about him.' And, with his mouth taking on an uncompromising grimness that made her wish she hadn't asked, he snapped, 'Nothing except that he was married.'

'Married?' It escaped Nadine on a shocked and trembling whisper, and with the feeling that she'd been thoroughly admonished she dropped her gaze to the photograph she was still holding, unable to sustain the hard blue intensity of his.

She could understand more clearly now his reasons for despising her. Indirectly he had created for his child the very same situation he himself had been born into, and he thought that she had been directly responsible for bringing it about. And without telling him the truth she had no hope of changing his attitude towards her, she realised, and desolately turning back towards the ladder, she murmured, 'I'll get that tea.'

CHAPTER FOUR

CAMERON drove back to London early on Monday morning, leaving before Nadine was even awake. She was relieved, in a way, when she came downstairs and realised that he had gone. While he was around she found herself struggling against her raging, guilt-ridden feelings for him, the attraction she had willed herself to ignore for all those years that he had been with Lisa but which had been smouldering beneath the surface, waiting to flare into life the first instant he touched her. Yet now that he had gone she felt surprisingly melancholy, and a little bit lonely too.

Fixing herself some breakfast, she sat down to browse through the newspaper that Cameron had bought in Bath at the weekend. Then, emptying the crumbs from the toaster on to a plate with the scraps of remaining toast that she hadn't eaten, she went outside to scatter them over the little sunny patch of lawn in the front garden, starting as someone uttered, 'Good morning, dear.'

A plump little lady with a basket over her arm was opening the gate, her bright checked shirt tucked into dark corduroy trousers that were secured around her ankles with bicycle clips.

'I'm Edna Bowles,' she informed Nadine, with a friendly glance from the younger girl's shining red hair, which was tied in a casual pony-tail, down over the still slender lines of her figure. 'From the village. I pop in once a week to make sure everything's all right with the house and to clean when anyone's been staying. Mr Hunter says you'll be leasing the place from him for the next few months, and that he'll want me coming in on a more regular basis.'

Nadine smiled, transferring the plate to her other hand to greet the woman formally as she introduced herself, deciding she was going to like Edna Bowles.

'Yes. I'm leasing it from him until the spring,' she enlarged, guessing that Cameron had told his cleaning lady that so that there wouldn't be any adverse speculation about her. Even so, she couldn't help feeling a ridiculous sense of insignificance in his life, being referred to merely as his tenant, even if—regardless of the child they had created—that was all she was to him. All, she realised, she would have to content herself with being.

It was Edna, she realised, though, who kept the place so spick and span, and after a while the two of them were chatting like old acquaintances.

'He's such a lovely man—that Mr Hunter,' Edna enthused over a cup of tea in the bright and sunny kitchen, her plump cheeks healthily pink. 'I didn't realise you'd moved in so soon. I thought it might be later in the week—only my neighbour said she noticed his car here most of the weekend...'

'Yes,' Nadine admitted quickly, aware that some of the villagers used the lane to walk their dogs. 'He had a lot of sorting out to do in the loft.' But she felt the colour invading her cheeks, and knew as she averted her eyes from Edna's what the cleaning lady would make of that.

'It probably needs doing. The place has hardly been touched since his old aunt died.' Swiftly the woman brushed over Nadine's embarrassment. It's hardly my business, was the unspoken message Nadine was relieved to grasp. 'Like her nephew, she was a strong, determined woman, but a bit of a hoarder, I suspect.'

She winked a twinkling blue eye at Nadine, who agreed with smiling wholeheartedness. Those delightful old things she had seen in the loft were testimony to that.

'He never once neglected her—at holiday times, birthdays. But he always came on his own...'

Edna's ponderous comment surprised Nadine. Surely Lisa couldn't have been *that* selfish in refusing to visit one of her husband's elderly relatives? she thought, wondering if her friend had ever been the person she'd imagined her to be. Edna's respect for Cameron, however, shone through like a beacon, assuring Nadine that, despite her own earlier conjecture, his privacy would be sacred to Edna Bowles.

She had brightened up by the time Edna had left, enough to start knitting a pair of baby bootees with the soft lemon wool she had bought the previous week, and then to prune a few rather wild-looking shrubs in the front garden.

The following day a tabby kitten came through the kitchen window while she was washing up, curled up in one of the sitting-room chairs and refused to move. When, after asking around the village the next morning in the hope of tracing its owner, her efforts proved futile, Nadine purchased the large portion of smoked mackerel she'd been craving since breakfast, raced back to the cottage, and with a, 'Come on puss,' to her new little resident, shared the freshly cooked meal with a very grateful cat.

It was a balmy evening and still light when she settled down to watch an interesting documentary, in the middle of which she heard the deep throb of a car engine coming along the lane.

Transferring the kitten that had been curled up on her lap on to a chair, she crossed to the open window. Cameron's Mercedes had just pulled up outside, and in spite of all the firm reminders she had been giving herself over the past days that he was still a married man, Nadine's heart gave an involuntary leap.

'Hello, Nadine.' His greeting was little more than dispassionate as she opened the door to him.

Her racing thoughts deduced that he had obviously come straight from his chambers, judging by the elegant dark suit he was wearing.

'One word-processor,' he stated, coming in and setting the large box he was carrying down on the sitting-room table. Then, looking about him, sniffing the air, he asked, 'What on earth have you been cooking? The place smells like Billingsgate Market!' That proud nose wrinkled in obvious distaste, though he was still managing to look amused.

'It was mackerel,' she said sheepishly, wishing she had been more extravagant with the air-spray—although she had had all the windows open. 'I had it for lunch.'

'Both of you?' Mouth quirking, his gaze had fallen on the kitten that was standing on the arm of the chair now, mewing for attention.

'You don't mind?' she uttered, shooting an anxious glance at him before going over and scooping the little creature up into her arms. 'You didn't actually say I couldn't have any pets...' Worriedly, she remembered that he'd shown no inclination to share any with Lisa. 'And I couldn't resist her. She just walked in yesterday—so I called her Tuesday.'

A smile flitted across his mouth, so fleetingly it might not have been there.

'You can do what you like,' he said phlegmatically, reaching out to pet the mewing little head. But in doing so his fingers accidentally grazed Nadine's cheek, a contact as sensual as it had been light, so that almost imperceptibly she flinched.

'Were you getting lonely?' It was a casual enough question. Why, then, was he looking at her as though he was trying to see into her very soul? Because he'd noticed that almost unconscious withdrawal?

Agitatedly, feeling sharp little needles piercing her skin through her fine blouse, she steadied the kitten's adventurous route to her shoulder and, going over to switch off the television set, said nonchalantly, 'No, not really.' Heaven forbid that he—or anyone else—should ever know how keenly she had felt his absence since he had left on Monday!

'Any other visitors?'

He meant men, and resentment showed in her eyes as she watched him toss down his jacket, watched the movement of muscle in his back beneath the fine shirt before he turned back to her, loosening his tie.

'No,' she responded, so adamantly that a thick, masculine eyebrow ascended in mocking acknowledgement. 'Only Edna,' she amended more calmly. 'She said she'll be in again tomorrow.'

'Good.' His mouth firmed as though in satisfaction. Due to her response to his question about having had no other visitors, she sensed, rather than Edna's increased endeavours. 'Have you eaten yet?' He pulled a wry expression, the strong angles of his face softening a little. 'I mean, since you stank the house out with that irresistible smelling lunch!'

'There's no need to rub it in! I didn't know you were coming, did I?' she defended in lightly remonstrative tones. 'I fancied it like mad. And no, I haven't had dinner yet, if that's what you meant.' A mischievous twinkle lit her green eyes and she was unable to resist adding, 'I was thinking of doing a curry—but I should warn you, I like it very hot. And perhaps vegetables with a nice garlic dip to start——'

'Forget it,' he drawled with a grimace. 'We're eating out tonight. A friend of mine owns a country club a few miles from here and I have to advise him on a small legal matter, so how soon can you be ready?'

'Half an hour?' Nadine suggested, trying to conceal the sudden reckless pleasure his invitation had evoked.

But in fact she was ready before he was, coming out of her bedroom having substituted blouse and jeans for a softly clinging green dress and almost colliding with him coming along the carpeted landing.

'Are you any good with a needle?' he enquired, tugging impatiently at one buttonless shirt-cuff, his foregone conclusion that she would sew it back on for him, regardless of his past treatment of her, making Nadine want to respond tartly, Yes, are you?

She bit back the provocative words, however, and went down to his aunt's sewing-basket, which she had noticed

under the old dresser in the sitting-room, returning with
a needle and silk thread.

'Are you going to take it off?' she uttered quaver-
ingly, because he was back in his own room, and the
sight of him standing there in that very masculine room,
with the gaping shirt exposing that equally masculine
chest, was producing little coils of tension in the pit of
her stomach.

'I don't think that will be necessary, do you?'

Of course it wasn't, she thought, flushing at the per-
ceptive mockery of his smile. And she was only sewing
a button on his shirt. So why did she feel as though her
fingers weren't actually in control of the needle? she
wondered as she threaded it through the pristine silk of
his cuff. Good heavens! If she didn't watch herself she'd
be sticking it into him, she realised, keeping her head
down so that the loose curtain of her hair hid the agi-
tation in her face as she tried to ignore how starkly that
feathering of dark hair on his wrist contrasted with the
immaculate white cuff, too conscious of the musky scent
that emanated from him, of his body warmth, of that
hard, masculine strength that had pressed her to the
bed...

'Ouch!' She felt him flinch and stammered her
apologies. 'What are you trying to do—inoculate me?'
he said drily. 'Or are you practising acupuncture in your
spare time?'

'I'm sorry.' She lifted her flushed face to the harsh,
handsome lines of his, seeing with intensifying discomfort the derision curving his lips, as though he'd
guessed what had brought about that little piece of
carelessness.

'There—that should do it.' She was glad when the task
was finished, then realised that she had forgotten to bring
up any scissors. When the thread didn't immediately yield
to her sharp, desperate little tug, she heard Cameron say,
'Here,' and drew in her breath as his hand suddenly
closed over hers and he dipped his head to catch the
silken strand between his teeth.

Nadine's heart seemed to stand still. Outside in the lane the repetitive cooing of a wood-pigeon impinged on the silence, but she barely heard it, alive only to the clean freshness of his hair, still damp from his shower, and the latent strength of that warm hand holding hers.

'Did Lisa sew all your buttons on like the dutiful wife?' she was uttering, through her need to say something, then wished she hadn't as his face, lifting so that it was level with hers, darkened with a whiplashing emotion.

'Is that what you think marriage is?' he enquired roughly. 'An assignment of servitude and duty?'

'Isn't it?' she suggested tremulously, wishing he'd let go of her hand. After all, her mother had worn herself out trying to please an unappreciative husband before he'd left her for a younger woman he'd considered more fun.

'Is that why you've decided not to bother?'

Piqued by his hardening tone, she managed to pull out of his grasp, only to feel those hard fingers snap around her wrist, sending alarm-bells jangling across her nerves.

'Is that why you're so anti-men?'

'I'm not anti-men!' Her hair moved like an angry red sea as she made a futile bid to free herself. Of course she had the sense to realise that not every man was like her father. 'I've known lots of men I've liked——'

'But not enough to father your child! So why pick on me, little virgin?' He made the word sound more denigrating than complimentary, making her recoil from the reminder. 'Because in me you found someone who could not only satisfy the needs of your purse—but also that profound sexual attraction——?'

'No!' All the depth of her humiliation went into that short, sharp denial, her lashes pressed hard against the wells of her eyes as though by not looking at him she could doubly repudiate the frightening implications of his statement. 'You were Lisa's husband, for goodness' sake!' Her lashes fluttered apart, her lightly shadowed green eyes meeting the penetrating depths of stormy sapphire. 'I never once entertained a single thought like that about you...'

'Never?' He uttered a short, disbelieving sound, and traitorously she felt the pulse in her wrist throb beneath the angry pressure of his thumb, saw him glance down, aware.

Unconsciously her gaze followed his. The delicate structure of her hand was a pale contrast to the dark strength of his, and glancing up she saw his mouth twist with bitter self-derision, his gaze lift to hers almost as if her thoughts had willed it to.

'What are you thinking, Nadine? That we fit superbly well together? Because, like it or not, darling, I'm the man you chose to sleep with—to impregnate you. The man to whom you were sobbing to unlock the pleasures of that lovely body. So despise me as you will—you *wanted* me inside you. And you can deny it as much as you like—you'll never convince me otherwise. Any more than I could convince myself—even when you were a stammering adolescent—that I was wholly unaware of you!'

Stunned, Nadine stared after him as he strode abruptly away from her, hearing the bang of the bathroom door he threw closed behind him.

What was he saying? That he had noticed her all those years ago? Noticed her, even though he had been on the surface of things, happily married to Lisa?

Well, of course he probably had, a little voice inside her accepted, without any undue pretensions. She wasn't immodest, but she knew she had been graced with more than her fair share of looks and a reasonable figure, and Cameron would hardly have been a man if he'd been blind to her sexuality, she thought with a fatalistic little sigh at the unwelcome degree of attraction she possessed for the opposite sex. Of course he'd noticed. But that didn't mean anything—not where any feeling for her was concerned anyway, she reminded herself firmly, and felt a little cloud settle over her as she went back downstairs to put the needle away.

*   *   *

The country club to which Cameron drove them seemed to be miles from anywhere, a charming old mansion-house nestling in the Mendip hills.

'You'll like Simon. We were at university together,' Cameron told her as they came along the tree-lined drive.' I'm not sure Molly's really his type, but you'll have to make your mind up about her.'

And Nadine did, put on an uneven footing from the outset when the bubbly-haired brunette announced presumptuously, before Cameron could even introduce her, 'And you must be the lucky Mrs Cameron Hunter.'

Later she explained that Simon hadn't had a chance to tell her that Cameron was bringing a guest, which was probably why, at that precise moment, Nadine had thought she'd heard the tall, unassuming-looking man beside her catch his breath.

'I—— No, I——' Awkwardly, she looked at Cameron, floundering for a tactful reply.

'Nadine's my assistant,' he conveyed smoothly and concisely, in a way that silenced the older woman, while granting her one of his most charming smiles.

'Oh,' was all she said, with an embarrassed little flush creeping along her cheekbones, but Nadine could feel Molly's gaze lingering on her face and figure, weighing up the sexuality that was perceptible even to her own sex, and Nadine could sense the unspoken question in the woman's eyes as they lifted from her to the dark, handsome barrister at her side and back to Nadine again. Was Cameron Hunter having an affair?

No, he took me to bed once and now I'm having his baby. But he doesn't love me or anything!

As they moved across the elaborately designed hall, she could feel her heart crying it out. No one would believe the situation if they knew! And why should she let an arrangement she had foolishly believed she was entering impartially and with her eyes wide open cause this empty chasm deep down inside of her—this wrenching pain across her chest? Had Cameron been right earlier? Had she not been as immune to him as she had fooled herself into believing? Had all the claims to detachment she'd made positively and often to herself, ever since he'd married, been only a sham—a suppression of feelings that couldn't be entirely extinguished, yet which she had had no right to feel?

She should have enjoyed the evening, because it was pleasant enough, but that startling analysis of her feelings earlier prevented her from relaxing entirely, although she hid the fact behind an amiable and glossy smile.

Simon Braith and his fiancée were nice—even if Molly's conversation was a little overwhelming at times. She was several years older than Simon, Nadine guessed, nearer forty than thirty, and, from something that was said, Nadine gathered that Molly was about to become his second wife, his first having deserted him for a saxophone player five years before.

She also learned far more from what was left unsaid of the deep respect and friendship that existed between the two men. And from the concerned regard that Simon directed at Cameron once or twice, when he wasn't looking, she wondered if Simon already knew about Lisa, if Cameron had confided in the other man. Although she couldn't really imagine Cameron confiding in—or needing—anyone.

'So you would advise me to try and settle out of court...?'

They were in the subdued ambience of the club's gourmet restaurant, and Simon was going over the main points of Cameron's opinion concerning a certain boundary dispute.

'Give me just a quarter of all that authority and know-how!' Molly enthused to Nadine across the table, clearly in awe of that ruthless intellect of Cameron's as she sent an admiring glance his way. 'How long have you been working for him?'

Molly's unexpected question caught Nadine off-guard, and with a soft movement of hair as she glanced up from the table, she answered evasively, 'Not very long.'

There was a quiet curiosity in the older woman's voice as she pressed, in more confidential tones, 'Simon said something earlier about you working for Cameron at the cottage. Handling his more private affairs.'

'That's right.' Nadine sent a casual glance his way, her gaze accidentally locking with the dark penetration of his, and a sharp little frisson rippled through her. 'He's writing a book.' She forced her attention back to Molly, though not before catching the disconcerting sagacity of his smile. 'On law reform. And as I've been a legal secretary...' She made a small gesture with her hands.

'The perfect combination!' Molly supplied with innuendo. 'How do you keep your mind on the job, with a boss like that popping in every...?' She paused, as though waiting for Nadine to furnish her with details of exactly how often Cameron visited his country home, and when she didn't, Molly went on, 'And if it isn't too imprudent to say it, Nadine, how does he keep his mind on *his*? You're as lovely as Cameron is—to use a rather obvious adjective—virile. I don't know about Lisa Hunter, but if it were me, I wouldn't allow Simon the pleasure of even employing a secretary who looked like you.'

Nadine laughed awkwardly. If only Molly knew! 'I don't think Cameron's the type of man who would bend easily to any woman's wishes,' she expressed, with more than a small degree of truth. Didn't she know it, from her own inevitable submission to his emotional blackmail when he'd insisted she move into the cottage?

'Well, I suppose that's what makes him so exciting and attractive to women.' Even though she was happily engaged to be married, Molly could obviously appreciate Cameron's smouldering sexuality. 'And I suppose she's beautiful and confident, and sure enough of him to know he'll always want her...' She gave a long, wistful sigh and then, her voice coming as though through a fog, asked, 'Are you OK, Nadine?' Concern lined Molly's forehead beneath the bubbly curls. 'What is it? Is it Simon's cigar?'

'No, no, I'm fine,' she uttered quickly, not wanting to make a fuss.

Only she wasn't. The thick Havana smoke, combined with the effort of trying to keep up a polite conversation with the effusive Molly, was affecting her more than she would have dreamt of admitting, bringing on the worst pangs of nausea she had known in days. She was glad when Molly, taking her at her word, turned and made some fatuous comment to Cameron about barristers being irresistible to women.

Dear heaven, she thought, let me make it through the rest of the evening without having to give in to this! But while she was listening to Molly's ceaseless chatter the scarlet and gold flock-papered walls seemed to quiver before her eyes. She blinked at the ruby-carpeted floor, which seemed to be mingling with the walls, with the ruby-coloured candles, blood-red against the stark white cloth, so that suddenly everything seemed to be swimming in a dizzying red sea.

And suddenly he was there beside her. She felt that strong hand on her shoulder, as firm as the deep and welcoming voice that was advising softly, 'Come along. We're going home.'

At that moment she couldn't speak—couldn't even think—was only afterwards immensely grateful to him that he had noticed—been aware. But somehow she was on her feet, leaning against the supporting reliability of his arm, and through a sickening haze she heard him telling the others, 'I'm taking Nadine back to the cottage. Thanks for dinner, Simon. I'll call you.'

And that was that, Nadine realised, envying that cool self-assurance that dispensed with the need for any further explanation. Or maybe he simply knew there was no time, because she was ill before she even made it to the car park, mercifully noticing the sign for the cloakroom just as they were approaching the main door and darting off as if her life depended upon it.

When she emerged some time later, pale and drawn and decidedly shaky on her feet, Cameron moved away from the wall on which he had been leaning, commenting with a grimace, 'Another minute and I'd have come in there after you. Come on. Let's get you home to bed.'

It sounded like paradise and, leaning heavily on his arm, she allowed him to guide her out to the Mercedes, glad when they were on the road.

'I'm sorry, Cameron,' she groaned, feeling wretched. Goodness! Why did she have to make such a fool of herself? 'The others... They must have thought——'

'No one would have thought anything,' he assured her with an edge of impatience to his voice. 'And if they did, what the hell does it matter anyway?'

It doesn't, not to you, she thought, wishing she possessed just an ounce of that superb male confidence as she watched the car's powerful headlights slicing through the darkness of the lonely Mendip lanes. Sheep moved in a field, shadowy figures caught in the glare of the lamps and a rabbit darted out from the side of the road, bemused for a second before it turned and darted back into the safety of the hedge.

'And don't use the headrest as a pillow,' she heard Cameron advising surprisingly gently as she closed her eyes, feeling better now, just very, very tired. 'A friend of mine did that once and tore a ligament when her head slipped off the rest. Put your head on my shoulder if you want to sleep.'

She didn't want to—use his shoulder, that was—but she couldn't keep her eyes open, and realising that it was sound advice she did as he had suggested, knowing a sharp little thrill from the soft wool of his jacket against her cheek.

'That's better,' she thought he murmured, and was aware of nothing else then until the car stopped and she heard the keys being taken out of the ignition.

'Come on, Nadine, wake up.' He was doing his best to rouse her, shaking her gently, his hand lightly tapping her cheek. 'Wake up, Nadine.'

She groaned against his hand, dreamily aware of the scent of cologne that still clung to his fingers, yet not altogether conscious of turning to press her lips against that strong, warm palm.

'Come on, Nadine. There's a good girl.' His voice sounded strangely hoarse, and he was shaking her a little more vigorously now, but she didn't want to wake up, to return to the cold reality of full consciousness and his ever-present contempt of her. She wanted to stay here, here in the warm cocoon of safety and feeling, here in his car.

'Cameron...' Lying half across his seat, she wasn't even aware that her face was upturned drowsily to his, or that his name had sounded like a plea from her warmth-induced lethargy—without inhibitions, a plea from her heart.

She heard the catch of his breath, then felt its release—a warm and sensual caress against her mouth. In a minute he would be kissing her! Her leaping senses roused her sufficiently to make her realise. It was, therefore, a brutal disappointment when he pressed her gently back against her seat and got out.

A thin sliver of moon silhouetted his dark figure as he came around the bonnet. 'Come on,' he said tightly, extending an arm to help her out of the car.

'Cameron, I...' Suddenly she felt ashamed. 'I didn't mean to——'

'I know.'

So why did he sound so exasperated with her? Exasperated and something else, she thought, deciding with a sharp twinge of recognition that it sounded remarkably like pity.

'I'm so tired...' Wrought with misery, she swayed against him as she took the first steps to the gate, every nerve firing into life as he suddenly lifted her up into his arms, saying in more compassionate tones, 'Come on. There's only one place for you.'

And that place was bed, she realised with a reckless tide of feeling when he was carrying her up the stairs, and with her face pressed into his shoulder she tried not to think of the tenderness he must have shown Lisa, not just in his lovemaking, but in other ways as well.

'You didn't have to carry me.' Why did she have to sound so disappointed? she thought, when he placed her down on her own single bed after pulling back the duvet. Surely she hadn't been hoping...?

'You weren't exactly...capable,' he said, sounding half-amused, his face in shadow because he had his back to the door and only the light from the landing afforded any illumination into her room.

'I haven't been drinking,' she protested to that dark countenance looming above her.

'No. Just drunk with fatigue.' In the half-light she saw his mouth quirk in an indulgent smile that made her heart miss a beat.

Every pulse started to race as he eased her gently towards him to deal with the zipper of her dress, a raw excitement making her weak, making her whisper breathlessly, 'Then why are you taking advantage of me?'

She heard him laugh quietly under his breath. 'Because you aren't in any position to be able to stop me.'

Heavens! Was he serious? Mentally she tried to shake herself out of this drugging lethargy, but her body didn't seem connected to her brain, and strong talons of need clawed at her stomach as she felt those capable hands tugging the dress down over her hips, felt their warmth around her ankles as he removed her sandals.

He was leaning over her now, sitting on the edge of the bed to unfasten her bra, and with feverish anticipation Nadine arched her back, making it easier for him, desire throbbing through her in a heated surge as he removed the wispy white lace, and she knew that even in this light he could see the betraying responses of her body.

Dear heaven! How could she have felt so ill an hour ago and now want a man with all the strength with which it was possible to want? she wondered, enthralled by the harsh beauty of his features, by the casual touch of his hands removing the last scrap of lace from her body, their roughened warmth a burning sensuality against her thighs.

'Cameron...'

His gaze, skimming briefly over her body, lifted to lock with hers, and she knew he could see the desire she could feel like a sultry heaviness pressing against her lids. Maybe she should have been embarrassed that he had undressed her, she thought, with an abandoned warmth stealing through her, but she wasn't. He was her only lover, had turned her into a whole woman, sowing his seed in her so that part of her soul was bound to him for eternity, and she needed him like the earth needed light and air and sunshine to survive.

'Cameron. I want you to know... I mean, I——' She was trying to find the right words to redeem herself in his eyes, but the gentle touch of his fingers against her lips prevented her from going on.

'Don't say anything that you'll regret in the morning,' he advised almost dispassionately, covering her with the duvet and leaving her nursing a frustration he must have been well aware of as he went out and down the stairs. She heard his retreating footsteps with a shame such as she had never experienced before.

Whatever had come over her? She groaned into the darkness. Surely she hadn't forgotten that he was still Lisa's husband? Why, then, had she allowed him to see just how much she wanted him? Thrown herself at him like that? He wasn't only married, she thought with shaming reasoning, he didn't even like her!

Her own cruel reminder forced hot, unbidden tears to squeeze out from beneath her lids. She wasn't the first woman to be having a baby by a man who didn't feel anything for her, who belonged to another woman, for that matter—even if the circumstances were rather un-usual. But that weekend when he had awakened her sexuality he had awakened something else in her as well, something stronger and more complex than the innocent fervour she had nursed for him during her teenage years. And it hurt. Dear God! It hurt so much!

She could hear him talking on the downstairs phone when she awoke the next morning.

'No,' he was saying to whoever was on the line, 'I shan't be in today. If there are any important messages for me ring them through to me here.'

His clerk, Nadine deduced with a little grimace, turning over in bed, but as full consciousness returned, with the usual dragging nausea, she remembered how unwell she had been at that club the previous night, and realisation dawned. He hadn't gone back to London because of her!

A sudden inner warmth eased the misery of feeling so physically rotten, and when she eventually made it downstairs she found Cameron setting up the word-processor in the sitting-room.

'Morning,' he greeted her, glancing up with a stray glimpse at Tuesday, who was on the chair beside him, playing with a dangling cable. 'How are you feeling?'

Stuffing her hands into the back pockets of her jeans, Nadine wrinkled her nose. 'Ask me again when these first three months are over,' she advised, her wan smile only emphasising the pale fragility of her features.

'At least that won't be too long now,' he stated with sound assurance, but there was concern in that dark regard before it dropped again to his task.

He was switching on the computer, tapping in something that brought a series of amber characters to the screen. Unobserved, Nadine watched him, noting the lean perfection of his hands, her eyes unconsciously going from the casual elegance of his clothes to his dark, tilted head and the absorbed concentration on his face, and a rush of emotion clogged her throat so that brokenly she uttered, 'You didn't have to stay.'

He spared her a glance as he switched off the computer, having satisfied himself that it worked. 'No,' he said, turning away.

But he had, she thought, wondering why he seemed colder this morning. Was it because of last night? she asked herself, with a simmering embarrassment over the way she had virtually invited him to make love to her boiling over into red-hot shame. Last night he had been tender, even if it had only been because she had felt so ill, and like a fool she had responded to his gentleness— a consideration he'd probably have shown towards anyone who'd felt as she had, while unconsciously she'd been hoping that it had meant something else.

It was obvious from his cool detachment this morning that he had realised it too, recognised the dangers of the situation. Issuing sensual threats against her in anger was one thing. Undressing her—touching her—when she was vulnerable and senseless enough to offer him an unwitting invitation to her body with a total disregard for his own vulnerability, was quite a different matter altogether.

He was married. With a strong effort of will she determined to keep reminding herself of that fact, striving for the same degree of integrity that had stopped Cameron from making love to her the previous night. He still loved Lisa. He didn't want to be involved with *her*. And, heaven only knew, *she* didn't want to do anything that could ultimately bring about their divorce! Attracted to him as she might be, she had no right to lead him on—or to entertain the sort of sensual fantasies about him that had been occupying her mind ever since the first time he had possessed her. That way lay danger for them both.

Nevertheless, it turned out to be a reasonably pleasant day. Around noon when she felt better, Cameron suggested a walk, taking her out across the fields and pointing out the familiar landmarks of his childhood: the old and gnarled oak tree he used to climb, the brook where he had fished for minnows, which had all but dried up, and as they passed the gate to a farm overlooking the village, he told her, 'That was where I crashed my first go-cart, straight into a steaming heap of freshly turned manure!'

'Never mind! You still came up smelling of roses!' Nadine laughed, finding it hard to picture him ever being in such a predicament. 'Were you banished from the house, or just scrubbed from head to foot before you were allowed back inside?'

A breeze ruffled his hair as they turned into the lane, a nostalgic smile appeasing the hard severity of his features. 'As I recall, I don't think I had any tea. I was made to strip in the garden and sent straight to bed for ruining the clothes my aunt had insisted my uncle burnt because she couldn't stand the smell!'

'Serves you right!' Nadine laughed again, her face alive with healthy colour, but tensed when his hand came over hers as she went to open the cottage gate, his other tilting her chin to the searching scrutiny of his gaze.

'That's better.' There was satisfaction in his regard of her glowing cheeks and the until recently absent lustre of her eyes. 'The fresh air's done you some good. You looked ghastly earlier.'

Is that the only reason you took me out? she thought, berating herself for feeling disappointed—for allowing every stupid nerve to tremble just from the lightest pressure of his thumb, and was grateful, then, for the distraction of little Tuesday who, having heard their voices, was gambolling down the path to meet them, her mews shrill and welcoming above the squeaking hinges of the gate.

Cameron had left for London later that evening, and Nadine didn't see him again for nearly three weeks. He telephoned, the day after he left, from his chambers, to ask in coldly clinical tones if she was all right. But he didn't come that weekend, or the next, and, sick at herself, Nadine realised why. There had been a tight-wire tension between them that last afternoon when he had been at the cottage, a tension born out of an already strong and testing sexual awareness of each other, which her behaviour the previous night had done nothing to temper. And now, because of it, he was doing the right thing and staying away, and though she knew she should have been glad, telling herself it was the best thing all round, she wasn't.

When another weekend arrived, and she realised he still wasn't coming, she had made arrangements for Edna to come in and feed Tuesday and taken herself off to Brighton, where her mother, having completed her convalescence, was staying, at the request of a widowed friend, for an extended holiday.

Dawn Kendall had appeared even stronger and brighter than when Nadine had seen her last, and her spirits had lifted when she'd seen her mother doing small tasks that previously had caused her so much fatigue and pain.

'Just make sure you don't overdo things, Mum,' Nadine had advised softly, taking the kettle from her mother who, in the absence of her friend who had gone shopping, had insisted on making some tea. 'You're looking better, but you've got to stay that way,' she had stressed, not wanting to consider, as she glanced back on that greying auburn head bent in setting cups on the kitchen table, how, without that operation, her mother could well have been totally bedridden by now. It would still be a matter of time, though, she'd realised, before the woman could resume a reasonably normal life again, and for that reason Nadine had refrained from saying anything about her pregnancy, deciding to wait until nearer the time, when it began to show.

The kitten was growing bigger every day too, driving Edna to distraction whenever she came to clean by leaping on to her duster out of the most unlikely places, and even once snuggling under a sweater in her shopping basket, so that she was halfway back to the village one morning before she heard a mewing on the bike behind her, and turned to see a startled little face peering up at her from behind the saddle.

'You'll get yourself lost, you little scamp!' Nadine chided laughingly, holding the kitten high above her

head. And then the thought suddenly struck her. Would
having a child be this much fun? She had never seriously
considered, until recently, the simple joys that having a
child might bring. She'd only thought about the rather
unnerving responsibility—and, at other odd times, the
birth. That was still too distant, though, to worry her
unduly, she thought, setting Tuesday down.

She looked ahead now with surprising impatience to
the day when she saw her baby's first smile, watched it
take its first wobbly steps. Also, that awful nausea wasn't
troubling her so much these days, and she was beginning
to feel fitter and healthier all round. Only that morning
Edna had remarked how lovely she was looking, and all
she'd been wearing was a loose top over a pair of faded
jeans! Her complexion was clearer than it had ever been,
and she knew there was an added lustre to her hair, and
that it was wholly because of the baby that was growing
inside her.

But where was its father? she wondered desperately as
she sat down at the word-processor to carry on typing
his book, because against all her firm resolutions she
wanted to see him, and it was no good trying to pretend
to herself that she didn't.

She could only deduce that after that last visit he had
decided to leave her alone; that perhaps he didn't trust
himself with her any more. But why hadn't he even
bothered to telephone her? she pondered, staring sightlessly at the active monitor. Had something happened
to him? Had Lisa come back?

A tearing pain across her chest almost took her breath
away, making her realise just how deeply she had allowed herself to become involved with him, when she'd
known from the start that it was unwise to; that any
feeling for him beyond that one passionate weekend in
Essex was strictly and thoroughly taboo. Naturally, if
he and Lisa had patched up their marriage she would
be happy for them—of course she would! she thought,
unable to deny the sudden intense anguish that sent
shivers through her body as she tried vainly to convince

herself that she'd remain unaffected. But why, for heaven's sake, hadn't he called?

It was much later the following evening that she heard his car pull up outside, and knew, as soon as she opened the door to him, that something was wrong.

CHAPTER FIVE

HE WALKED in with only the curtest of greetings, his mouth set in such grim lines that a sudden, swift pain tore viciously through Nadine.

Had he made it up with Lisa? An anguish she refused even to acknowledge throbbed desolately along her veins. And why was he looking through her like that? Was it something to do with the baby? Had he repaired his marriage and now decided to fight her for guardianship after all?

Fear clutched her heart as she watched him stride into the sitting-room, flop heavily down into an easy chair.

He looked tired, immensely so, she thought—puzzled—yet somehow still magnificent, in a casual shirt and dark trousers. But those darkly circled eyes were raking over her as if he had never seen her before. 'What is it?' she said, fear clogging her throat. 'What's wrong?'

Silently he held out a rolled newspaper. 'It's all in there,' he said, and despite his grim appearance his tone was surprisingly level. 'Page four.'

Nadine looked at him, frowning, turning to the page he had referred to. She had to scan it several times before she realised which column it was he wanted her to see and her blood seemed to freeze with a numbing co-alescence as she read the small headline: 'British Barrister's Wife Killed in South of France.'

'*Lisa*?' She spoke in an uncomprehending whisper as, disbelievingly, her eyes skimmed the few following brief lines. 'When? When did it happen?' she asked, unable to digest barely anything she had read; only that Lisa—her friend—had crashed her car, killing herself and the one male passenger she had been with.

'Last weekend.' Cameron's tone was flat. 'She was way over the limit. They both died instantly.'

'Why didn't you tell me before?' she uttered, dazed with shock, her face bloodless against the shining auburn of her hair.

She saw his gaze lift from her hands, which were trembling now, back to the stark emotion in her blanched features.

'I knew it would be a shock to you,' he said quietly, all emotion concealed behind that façade of imperviousness. 'You had a longer standing relationship with her even than I did. It wasn't something I wanted to tell you over the phone.'

'No,' Nadine murmured automatically. She couldn't believe it! Lisa dead? Killed through being over the limit.

'I've just got back from France.' With his elbow resting on the arm of the chair, wearily Cameron rubbed his forehead. 'The identification. The arrangements for the funeral...'

The newspaper rustled as she let it drop absently to her side. It must have been hard for him, she thought. Far harder than he was allowing to show.

'Of course,' she said quietly, guessing that the next few days would be even more painful for him. With a sudden, torturing guilt she half expected some comment from him about her, Nadine, not being totally blameless for Lisa's fate, bracing herself for some bitter condemnation. And as if that instinct of survival had somehow broken through her numbness, stimulated her thinking processes again when nothing had been forthcoming, she murmured tentatively, 'It says she had a passenger.'

'Yes.' His gaze caught and held hers, his scrutiny so intense that she wanted to look away and couldn't. 'Yes,' he said again, exhaling heavily, bringing his hand down so hard on the arm of the chair that it made Nadine flinch.

'Why are you looking at me like that?' he enquired, his tones hard, almost reproaching.

Nadine swallowed as he got up and came towards her, suddenly feeling as guilty over concealing Lisa's affair as if she had been the unfaithful party.

'You knew, didn't you?' he murmured then, with a steely quietness.

Doubly shocked, Nadine clutched the newspaper in front of her with both hands now. 'Wh—what do you mean?' she stammered evasively.

Cameron slipped his hands into his trouser pockets, half turning to look down into the fireless grate.

'What were you trying to do?' Unexpectedly he sliced a hard glance in her direction, causing her heart to bang against her ribs. 'Spare my feelings?' His humourless laugh bore the cutting edge of a bitter self-derision and nervously Nadine moistened her lips. How did he know?

'There was a letter in Lisa's room—the room she was sharing with the man who was in the car with her. Oh! She was very prolific!' he ground out between clenched teeth, and with such raw emotion that Nadine wondered with a chilling shudder what Lisa could possibly have written. That she'd told her, Nadine, that she was having an affair even while she was living with Cameron? That they'd laughed about it as if it was some schoolgirl secret? Oh, God, don't let him believe that! she prayed, not wanting to think badly of Lisa but uncertain any more of what her old friend could have been capable of.

'She must have been intending to post it that day,' Cameron was continuing, 'because the envelope was sealed and stamped. She was virtually begging me to divorce her. She presumed I already knew about her friend Max from you—that you would have told me,' he said on a hesitant, almost contemplative note. 'Apparently she saw you in the car park of the sports centre one lunchtime when she was with him, and wasn't sure at the time whether you'd seen her or not—until I told her later that day that you'd been to see me to tell me you were keeping the baby. It seems—unlike myself, who wasn't entrusted with the whole truth——' he sounded annoyed—angry '—she easily put two and two together.

'She didn't walk out because you were keeping the baby. In fact her letter indicated that in the circumstances she couldn't help feeling relieved. The only reason she left was because she thought you would have told me everything—that her affair was about to be blown wide open.' Deep grooves were etched around his mouth, hardening that uncompromising jaw. 'She was so determined to finish our marriage off that she'd written that if I didn't give her a divorce she'd try to seek one...' His hesitation brought Nadine's eyes to his with a questioning intensity. 'By trying to make some case out of my adultery with you.'

His revelation was like a physical blow and she took an unsteady step back, as if to lessen its impact.

'No,' she uttered, the small negation strung with wounded disbelief.

'Why didn't you tell me?'

He was referring to the other man she had seen Lisa with that day, and she wasn't sure whether it was commendation for her silence or reproof that glimmered in the depths of his eyes.

'How could I?' she contested, flopping down into the opposite chair, absently letting the newspaper fall to the floor. She felt like crying—over Lisa—over her total betrayal of their friendship—but tears wouldn't come. 'It wouldn't have been right to... to do anything that could have resulted in destroying your marriage altogether.'

'You kept quiet about it——' something close to amazement crossed his face, laced the deep timbre of his voice '—for the sake of my marriage?'

She nodded. 'Yes,' she said quietly, unhappily, and gasped as Tuesday, ever on the look-out for a convenient lap, leaped up on to her knees. Little claws dug into her flesh through her thin summer skirt as the cat circled around for a comfortable spot to settle, but Nadine almost welcomed the pain, welcomed it as a diversion from the shock and numbing hurt she felt inside.

'And that's why you decided to keep the baby.' It was a pure statement of fact. He understood now.

Nevertheless, unconsciously stroking the kitten, which had suddenly curled up with its little head in the curve of her arm, she uttered, 'Would you have handed over your child in those circumstances?'

His eyes held hers for a long time, dark with a turmoil she could only assume was grief. 'It is my child,' he said quietly. There was nothing reprehensive or covetous behind that remark, just simple confirmation of the truth. But then he turned away and walked over to the window, staring out at the late sun turning the languid trees to flame in the field opposite. 'You should have told me,' he said on a shuddering breath.

Why? If you'd known she was with another man would it have stopped you wanting her? she thought poignantly.

Staring up at the taut structure of his back, she could feel the raw emotion in him as acutely as her own, though, of course, his pain had to be a whole world stronger than hers.

She ached to go over to him, comfort him, put her arms around that tight, lean waist and cry into that strong, muscular back, I need you. Please hold me. But she didn't dare. He was grieving deeply and privately for another woman. No matter how bound she was to him because of the baby, he was still in love with Lisa, and no amount of wanting or needing on her part could alter that.

The funeral took place several days later, a dreary, cold day when it rained in a steady, relentless deluge from morning til night.

Cameron had wanted as private an affair as possible, and so the gathering in the little churchyard was small. Lisa's widowed mother, down from the North with her new husband, a couple of distant relatives and a rather striking brunette about the same age as Nadine who sent her several subtle yet speculative glances, she noticed, and that was all.

Cameron had seemed to take it all with a far greater degree of calm than she had felt, Nadine reflected later. Because although her own feelings had been locked inside of her, tears refusing to come, it had been emotional torture standing at the graveside of the young woman she'd believed to be her friend. She'd wondered if Lisa's mother had known of the break-up of her daughter's marriage, and guessed she probably had. Nevertheless, if the woman had noticed her son-in-law lending a supportive arm to the pale, slim creature at his side, she would probably have thought nothing of it beyond Cameron's duty to her daughter's closest friend, unaware—as she surely must have been, Nadine decided— that she was expecting his baby. While she, herself, didn't know how she would have got through the day without him.

He had insisted on taking her back to her flat as soon as it was over, aware, even without being told, how faint she had started to feel.

Later, though, needing something to do, she cleaned and dusted the place in readiness for the new sub-tenants, who were moving in the following week, packing up the remainder of her small, personal belongings so that she was ready and waiting when Cameron returned to drive her back to the cottage the following day.

Neither of them spoke much during the journey down and Cameron seemed as darkly aloof as the blanket of thick sombre cloud hanging dismally over the motorway. The countryside, though, had weathered the storms far more gracefully than the city, she was somewhat cheered to notice, because by the time they reached the Somerset village the fields were glistening beneath a sun that shone dramatically through the heavy clouds, and the raindrops on the early-changing leaves of one of the horse-chestnuts in the lane as they turned into it were sparkling like amber crystal.

'Where's Tuesday?' Cameron commented, looking round the sitting-room as Nadine turned on the gas fire.

'I left her with Edna.' Chilly in the light skirt and blouse she'd worn back from London, gratefully she watched the blue flames leaping into life, thinking how cold and empty the cottage seemed without the cat. 'I didn't think she'd want to be left on her own too long—and I wasn't sure what time I'd be back. I'll walk down and pick her up some time this afternoon.' And later she might walk off this dreadful depression, she thought, feeling the pain of unshed emotion like a crushing weight against her chest.

'Why don't you put the kettle on?' he suggested gently. 'And I'll pop down to the village and get her.'

'Would you?' A spark lit her eyes, his suggestion elevating her spirits a little. As he'd known it would, she thought fifteen minutes later when he returned just as she had finished making the tea, and pulled the mewing little creature out of its basket.

'There you are. There's your mum.' He wasn't above making small talk with a cat, she realised, with a tug of reluctant warmth for him as he handed her the kitten. Although his fingers accidentally brushed hers, evoking such a desperate need in her to feel the comfort of his arms around her that she looked quickly down at Tuesday, stammering her thanks, afraid her feelings were too apparent in her face. Because the truth was that since Lisa's death she had felt more remote from him than at any time before, at a distance that was only serving to compound her misery as he suddenly turned away, saying with a cool impartiality, 'Now, where's this leak you wanted me to look at?'

Ten minutes later he was fixing that, too—his watch discarded on the drainer, lying virtually on his back under the sink to replace a worn washer while Nadine watched, admiring his capable strength and the long, lean lines of his body, as she sipped her tea, and distant thunder rumbled ominously across the sky.

Later, watching him gathering up some books and papers he was taking back to London, Nadine felt the strength of her loneliness threatening to overcome her, trying not to imagine what it would be like after he'd gone.

'Are you sure you won't stay for something to eat?' She strove to conceal the desperate plea in her voice and only just succeeded.

'No.' It was a very positive refusal. He didn't need her unburdening any emotion on him, she thought with a gripping, tearing anguish on reminding herself that he harboured a more profound feeling of his own. 'If I need to, I'll get something on the road.'

He didn't need to say any more. He wanted to be alone—naturally—with his memories of Lisa. For now, the fact that she, Nadine, was carrying his child, was only secondary to him.

'Of course.'

He was slipping on a casual jacket because rain was threatening outside. The odd flash of lightning filled the room and each roll of thunder was responding with increasing vehemence, so that in a desperate bid to keep him there unwittingly she was uttering, 'You'll be all right in the storm?'

His mouth lifted at one side and he came over to her, placing his hands on her shoulders, their warmth penetrating her thin blouse.

'My dear Nadine, carry on like this and I'll start to imagine you're worried about me.' He gave an imitation of a smile, causing her breath to lock in her lungs when he suddenly bent his head and pressed his lips lightly against her forehead. 'I'll be in touch,' he said softly, and then he was gone, leaving her with only that indefinable scent of him clinging to her nostrils, and the sound of rain spattering heavily on the path as the front door opened briefly for a few moments and then closed again.

It was the sound of his car pulling away that pressed home her crushing isolation. Alone now, there was nothing to rein in the emotion she'd been holding in check over the last few days, and suddenly it was pouring from her like water from a burst dam.

Blinded by tears, she collapsed beside the settee with her head on her arms, her convulsive sobs stifled by the cushions and the crash of the thunder overhead. Her misery seemed eternal, spasms shaking her body, but it was more for herself than anything else that she was crying, because of all she had been through during the past few months with her mother, Lisa, Cameron's contempt and continuing indifference towards her, and the endless futility of her feelings for him. And then, through her weeping and the raging storm, she thought she heard another sound.

Red-eyed, her hair falling untidily around her face, she lifted her head and turned round, thinking it must be Tuesday. Her sobs were broken only by a small shocked gasp to see Cameron standing there by the door.

His hair was ruffled by the wind and there were dark patches on his jacket from the heavy rain. His expression, though, was a mixture of surprise and painful intensity as he regarded the tears running down her face and the next moment, she wasn't sure how, she was in his arms, sobbing now from the sheer joy and comfort of his protective warmth that was suddenly enveloping her.

'Oh, my brave, beautiful girl, don't cry.' His voice was thick with emotion as he stroked the soft silk of her hair. 'Hush, hush,' he murmured deeply, and she thought she heard his voice tremble, every part of her welcoming the lips that were caressing the soft, damp curve of her jaw, her cheek, the salty dampness of her wet lashes.

She groaned against his throat, uttering a small, helpless sound as he pulled her head back and his mouth suddenly turned urgent, to clamp savagely over hers, his hands holding her head, fingers tangling in her hair while his desperate, hungry kisses devoured her.

'I need you, Nadine. God knows! I need you!' His words were as ragged as his breathing, torn from the agony of his wanting, and eagerly she pressed herself to him with a surge of naked longing, nails digging into the damp fabric covering his shoulders, every nerve aching for the fulfilling intimacy she craved.

Tomorrow she would regret it. From somewhere in her subconscious came the warning she tried to heed and failed, hearing only what her heart and soul and her body were telling her; that she had been made for this man, that there would never be another. He was the father of her baby, and no matter what happened tomorrow he was here—now—and she needed him!

He was tugging her blouse out of the waistband of her skirt and she sucked in her breath from the heated desire his hands inflamed as they found the soft, silken contours of her body, inciting her own need to touch him, her hands to slip inside his open jacket, pull at his shirt in their quest for the velvet warmth of the flesh they ached to feel beneath.

She heard his breath shudder through his lungs and, above the electric storm raging overhead, his husky, 'For goodness' sake, let's go to bed!'

She couldn't speak—too overwhelmed by desire to give him an answer. But he didn't even wait for one, sweeping her off her feet and carrying her upstairs as he had done that night three weeks ago, only this time when he placed her down on her bed he didn't withdraw from her, but came down heavily beside her. With hungry impatience he tore at the impeding barrier of her clothes, at the same time shedding his own, his lips and hands claiming each part of her bared softness with untamed, almost ravening urgency, bringing her straining towards him, her body glorying in the feel of those hands it knew and had craved for so long.

'Your body's softer—rounder...' With a sudden gentle possessiveness his hand strayed down her ribcage to the small mound between her hips. 'Because of me...'

She uttered a tremulous sigh at the shuddering emotion in that deep voice and wanted to cry out when he dipped his head and his lips touched the spot where his hand had lain; to cry out that she wanted him, needed him, that she loved him!

She acknowledged it openly now, but she kept it to herself, sobbing out instead with the sudden, pleasurable torment of his mouth against her breast that made her body stiffen with excruciating need, her desire coil deep within the heart of her femininity.

It was still only mid-afternoon, yet the room was almost in darkness because of the storm. She could hear the rain lashing against the window, see through closed lids the lightning's trembling brilliance; her cries of sweet torture were lost in the crack of thunder immediately overhead that seemed to rock the earth.

And then he was taking her, with one forceful thrust of his body, driving everything from her mind but the ravaging joy of total oneness with him as she welcomed him into her in a wild explosion of the senses that was fiercer than the storm. His body was hard and heavy on hers and she rose to meet its strength, sobbing from the raw, throbbing pleasure that was engulfing them both, from the shocking violence of their aggressive hunger for each other which was only appeased by the blinding orgasm that finally left them sated and spent.

After a while Cameron got up without a word and started to dress, causing Nadine to stir from her comforting lethargy.

'You aren't going?'

'Yes.' He didn't even look at her where she lay, propped up on an elbow, and only the faint rumble of thunder filled the silence, distant—miles away now. 'I only came back because I forgot my watch. I'm sorry. I shouldn't have let that happen. I didn't intend it to.'

His words stabbed her like the sharp point of steel. 'I know,' she accepted flatly, wondering how she was ever going to survive this pain. Of course he blamed himself—regretted it now—because he hadn't really wanted *her*. He was mourning the woman he had loved and lost—despite her cruel infidelity—and making love to *her* had been just a bitter-sweet release from the pain.

'It wasn't all your fault,' she said, trying to ease his guilt. But who was going to ease her own agony over the knowledge that she was just a substitute for Lisa? 'Don't feel too bad about it. We both needed a release.' Quickly she rambled on, through a desolation that was even more crushing than before, adding with all the self-command she could muster, 'It didn't mean anything...'

His eyes seemed almost to impale her as he pulled his shirt on over his trousers. 'No?' he challenged quietly—brutally—that sceptical movement of an eyebrow making her defences rush to the fore as he started fastening his buttons. Surely he couldn't have guessed how she'd given her very soul with that sweet, wild abandonment of her body?

'No,' she emphasised with a feigned composure, pulling the duvet up around her as though it could protect her from him—from herself.

'Of course,' he accepted, with a strange inflexion in his voice, though the ghost of a smile tilted his mouth as he came back to the bed and sat down. 'I forgot how generously you give yourself when you're making love. You make a man forget everything in the sweet oblivion of that lovely body.' And quietly, 'Thank you for that, Nadine.'

She tensed, inhaling the erotic musk of his body as he leaned across and, despite his earlier admission of regret, kissed her gently on the mouth, then traced its full, swollen outline with his thumb.

'Why is a woman's mouth so soft after she's been crying?'

Of course, he would know.

'The voice of experience?' she queried, unable to avoid sounding bitter, and couldn't help wondering how many women he had known before he'd married Lisa—how many had shed tears over him, as she knew she would, eventually.

With his arms on either side of her now, as if he could see into her soul, quietly he said, 'I'm not that much of an ogre, Nadine.'

She felt the sting of tears behind her eyes, but held them in check. 'Oh, yes you are,' she whispered.

He was so close that his breath was stirring her hair, and the warm musk emanating from him was a potent, heady torture to her aching senses. She felt the treacherous trickle of desire seep along her veins and knew that if he touched her again it would become a torrent and she would drown in its merciless power. But then a peculiar scratching sound had them both turning towards the wardrobe, the sight of Tuesday squeezing out from underneath resulting in a mutual exclamation of laughing surprise.

'She was frightened by the storm!' Nadine realised sympathetically, because the last time she'd seen the cat it had been curled up asleep in the sitting-room chair, and colour stained her cheeks as she realised how everything had been forgotten in their urgency for each other, in the mutual heat of their physical desire. 'Oh, no!' It was a little cry of despair as the cat, leaping on to the dressing-table, knocked over a vase of dried flowers in its haste to get out of the room.

'I think whoever owned her before must have objected to her being in the bedroom,' Cameron commented drily, getting up, the supple leanness of him causing a sharp twinge in her loins as she watched him retrieve the vase and flowers from the carpet.

'You could be right.' Clutching the duvet, Nadine groped around for the robe she knew she'd left on the bed, frowning as her fingers found the satiny garment on the floor beside it.

'Well, what did you expect?' His astute observation made her blush, his silent appreciation of her as she pulled the dove-grey satin over her nakedness making her feel strangely self-conscious. She was glad when he looked away, down at the little plaster vase in his hand, saying, 'It must have hit the edge of the stool before it landed on the carpet. I'm afraid it's badly chipped. I could try and fix it for you, but I don't think it's going to look quite the same as it did.'

'No, that's all right,' she said, belting her robe as she got up, because every second he stayed was agony, and though she wanted him there, she wanted him to go too. 'Put it in one of the drawers for now.'

All she wanted to do was get away from him, wash away the lingering traces of him from her body—forget how incredibly he made love. But she knew she'd never be able to do that. Stumbling over the tumbled folds of the duvet as she was making for the bathroom, she heard his, 'What the...?' The surprise and puzzlement in his voice making her glance round.

He had put the vase in the drawer, as she had requested, but now he was taking something out. Dismayed, Nadine realised what it was. The last invoice she had received from the convalescent home! It had arrived the day he had come and told her about Lisa, and she'd forgotten she'd stuffed it in there, too shaken at the time to think about filing it away with the others.

'I thought I told you to...' He was frowning down at the piece of paper in his hand and it suddenly dawned on Nadine what he was thinking. He thought she was having some sort of treatment he didn't know about, when he'd insisted on footing the bill for all her antenatal care himself. That was until he said, 'Dawn Kendall? Your *mother*?'

Those dark brows knitted in increasing bewilderment, and knowing that it was pointless trying to keep it from him any longer, Nadine took a deep breath and explained.

'Mum didn't want anyone to know how ill she was,' she finished with a little sigh.

'So you kept it to yourself.' Clearly he was stunned by the news as he glanced down again at the invoice. 'It must be costing you a fortune...' He looked up then, his words tailing away, clarity dawning in his eyes. His whispered expletive was unrepeatable. 'You mean, you agreed to go to bed with me—to have a baby—so that you could...' His expression showed hard disbelief. 'Why the hell didn't you at least tell *me*?' he rasped.

Nadine subsided on to the bed again. 'And what was I supposed to say? Please, Cameron, could you give me

X amount of cash to pay my mother's hospital bills? I don't think I'll ever be able to pay it back—but you won't mind that, will you?' She pulled a twisted little face. 'You weren't exactly the approachable type. Anyway, it was Lisa I thought was my friend, and I knew she didn't have an income of her own—and even if she had, I couldn't have just asked her for the money——'

'But you could have told me afterwards—after we——' Admonishingly his gaze ran over her dishevelled red hair, down over the clinging satin that emphasised her soft curves and which had fallen open to expose one creamy, slender leg. 'Good grief! If intimacy like we shared doesn't inspire confidences . . .!'

'How could it?' she argued, with a challenging lift of her chin. 'It was only——' She had been going to say 'an arrangement', but was afraid that if she did her voice might betray just how much it hurt to say it, so quickly she changed course, saying instead, 'You bullied me from the beginning, and I thought that if you realised how ill Mum was you'd try and use it against me. Besides, even if I hadn't promised her that I wouldn't tell anyone and you'd given me the money, how do you think she would have felt, knowing she was in that hospital through some outsider's charity?'

'Far less appalled, I would imagine, than finding out just how her daughter did raise the cash.'

'You won't tell her?' Panic lit her eyes as she watched him toss the invoice back into the drawer. 'You won't, will you?' she uttered, unable to contain the pleading in her voice.

'Doesn't she know yet?' Astonishment showed in his face as he turned back to face her. '*Anything* about the baby?'

'No.' It was a small pained whisper.

'So what—and when, exactly,' he said tightly, 'are you going to tell her?'

'I don't know.' She stood up, her arm lying across her waist, nibbling apprehensively on a nail.

She could feel his censuring disapproval in the ragged breath he drew. 'A real creature of evasion and subterfuge, aren't you?' he chided, sounding exasperated with her.

'No, I'm not,' she defended wearily. 'I'm going to tell her some time.' She just didn't know when, yet, or exactly how she was going to do it.

'You'd better make it soon.'

She didn't need him to tell her that, any more than she wanted to think about it at that moment.

Outside, on the landing, Tuesday was scampering about, chasing some imaginary prey.

'Well.' He inhaled heavily, and now some dark emotion gave a stark, bleak look to his features. 'Is there anything else you've been keeping from me, Nadine?'

Only that I love you. It took all her strength not to say it, only the knowledge that that tortured look in his eyes had no bearing on any feeling for her locking her in painful silence, so that all she could do was shake her head before dragging herself away from him to the bathroom.

CHAPTER SIX

DURING the next few weeks Nadine's health blossomed into radiance. Her pregnancy was making itself more evident too, she realised, the morning she had to alter the waistband of her favourite trousers before she could get them on.

Also, Dawn Kendall had written to say that she was feeling fit enough now to return home. Consequently, the day she finally left Brighton, Nadine packed Tuesday off to Edna's and caught the first train back to London, telephoning Cameron as soon as her mother was settled back in to let him know what was happening.

'Mum's come home, so I'll be staying here in London with her for a few days if you ... need me for anything,' she said, but hesitantly, from the aching knowledge that despite the intimacies they had shared she still couldn't say she had any claim to his affections. Though his visits, since that day after the funeral, had been regular enough, she had sensed a cool restraint in him towards her ever since.

It was therefore a surprise when he answered in mildly mocking tones, 'Of course I need you, Nadine,' making every nerve pulse with the anguished reminder of him saying the same thing before their reckless lovemaking that day in the storm. 'How is your mother now? Well enough to be left on her own for a while?'

'I'm sure she is. I'm just staying to make sure she doesn't do too much all at once,' she answered, breathless from the impetuous responses of her body.

'Good. In that case you can come up and meet me for lunch tomorrow,' he was stating, with that bold assurance that said the matter was already settled. 'And, Nadine ...'

'Yes?'

'Try to relax a little. Not just while you're playing nursemaid—but with me. You sound like an apologetic client with a coiled spring inside of her. Remember you're having a baby. Getting uptight could affect the poor little mite's psychological balance for life.'

But that's how you make me feel, Nadine thought, grimacing, although his paternal protectiveness gave an involuntary tug on her emotions so that she had to struggle to say lightly, 'Hardly, Cameron. It does have some degree of protection from all we're likely to throw at it. Also it's a Hunter. That surely gives it more than its fair share of immunity to the outside world.'

There was silence while he digested that little piece of sarcasm. Then, with an almost amused calmness that showed he was in no way perturbed, he said softly, 'Goodbye, Nadine.'

Which put her in her place good and proper! she thought, feeling the bite of frustrated tears behind her eyes. Nothing she did or said could touch him beyond the boundaries of a devastating sexual passion. And even that, she reminded herself wretchedly, was against his will!

He was waiting on the steps of his chambers when she went up to meet him the following day.

Exuding that air of ruthless confidence, he smiled as soon as he saw her, the powerful lines of his physique tempered into sleek elegance by the expensive tailoring of his suit.

'You're late,' he said. 'I was getting worried about you. Did you have problems with the trains?'

She murmured a thready, 'Yes,' out of breath not only because she had been rushing, but because the sheer impact of his vital magnetism was making her pulses race. And she wasn't thinking about the trains, only about how cruelly beautiful he was, and how the early autumn sun streaked fire through his thick black hair.

'That's not good.' It was her dashing about he obviously disapproved of, she realised, rather than her being
late, but her starved senses were keeping her from feeling
anything but the strong arm that was suddenly lying
across her shoulders as they moved across the quiet inn
square towards the restaurant.

'I'm free this afternoon,' he told her after they had
finished a superb two-course lunch and he was paying
the bill. 'Do you have anywhere particular to go?' And
when she shook her head he said, 'Good,' pocketing his
wallet and guiding her out into the mellow afternoon
sunshine. 'I have something to do, but it won't take long.
Then we can take you home.'

She started to protest that it wasn't necessary, but he
was already hailing a taxi. Besides, she knew him well
enough now to realise that when he made up his mind
about something he was as immovable as a pyramid,
and so she remained silent, expressing only a small el-
ement of surprise when he helped her from the cab on
to a garage forecourt.

'Are you having your car serviced?' she asked, looking
enquiringly up at him as he led her past the petrol pumps
around the side of the building. 'Not exactly,' was all
he responded with, so she didn't pursue the point, wondering if he might be having some accident damage
beaten out that he was too proud to admit to as he turned
to a passing mechanic and said, 'My name's Hunter. You
telephoned me earlier about the car.'

Nodding, the man disappeared, pulling up beside them
a few minutes later in a little silver saloon. He got out,
tossing Cameron the keys.

'Here. Take it, it's yours.' Amazingly Cameron was
holding out the keys to Nadine. 'Only, don't exceed the
limit—and *don't* go leaving it unlocked and unattended
until we get it transferred into your own name, or I could
lose my no-claim bonus—and for that I'd have to put
you over my knee.'

Dumbfounded, she stared at him. 'I—I couldn't!' she breathed, too flabbergasted to rise to those last provocative remarks.

'You can and you will,' he threw back determinedly. 'What are you afraid of? Being further committed to me, Nadine? I'm afraid you made that choice a long time ago. Here.' He thrust the keys into her hand. 'Get in and get the feel of the controls while I settle things with the manager. Then you can drive me to your mother's, and from there I'll get a taxi back.'

It was useless protesting—against any of his demands—and so she slid into the car. It wasn't straight out of the factory, but as good as, she thought, inhaling the newness of the carpets and upholstery, excitement singing through her with just the slightest twinge of nerves. She hadn't driven since she'd passed her test.

'Right then. All set?'

Was she? Mentally she grimaced as she turned the key in the ignition, conscious of how big Cameron appeared as he strapped himself into the small saloon.

'You might need that,' she joked, 'if I wind up in a ditch!' And then, as what she'd said suddenly dawned on her, 'Oh, God! I'm sorry.' She couldn't look at him as she fumbled with the gear-stick. How could she have been so thoughtless, saying something like that?

'I was hoping you could drive it around Somerset first,' Cameron remarked after what seemed an eternity. 'As it is, you've got London traffic to contend with— which probably—in the long run—is the best way of breaking you in.'

'You make me sound like a horse.' Her smile was amiable—if a little tense—relieved as she was that he had brushed over her tactless little indiscretion with his seemingly usual calm.

'I suppose there's some similarity.'

Out of the corner of her eye she caught his grimacing amusement, shooting back with feigned outrage, 'Like what?'

'Ooh…you need feeding—and a warm blanket thrown over you at night.' Unsettlingly, she felt his gaze slide down over her loosely belted green silk top and matching skirt. 'And you've got great legs.'

'Thanks!' she laughed sarcastically. 'Anything else you want to comment upon?'

'Not that's immediately on view. And keep your mind on what you're doing,' he advised quietly as she pulled out of the garage into the disconcertingly busy flow of traffic, although he didn't need to tell her again.

If she wanted to prove to him that she was a fully competent driver, then even more she wanted to prove it to herself. And in fact she took to it very well, she adjudicated a little later, deciding it wouldn't be too immodest to give herself a little mental pat on the back as she filtered across into a right-hand lane with comparative ease.

'I take it your mother knows now about the baby?' His sudden, heart-plummeting question brought her too close to the car in front, so that she had to brake hard and stalled. His rasped, 'For goodness' sake, watch your driving!' shook her into realising how easily she could be unsettled as she spent a few embarrassing seconds getting started again. 'Well?' he pressed, after giving her sufficient time to regain her self-composure.

'No.' She glanced in the rear-view mirror, her already sinking confidence taking a further dive when she saw the driver of the car behind gesticulating rudely at her.

'What the hell do you mean—no?'

'I mean, I haven't yet.'

'Why ever not?' He sounded appalled. And then, decisively, 'I think the three of us had better have a little chat this afternoon.'

'No!' Dread filled her eyes as she darted a glance across at him, her knuckles whitening from where her fingers were tensely gripping the wheel. 'Not today!' she stressed, wanting to put it off, as she had been doing ever since he had raised the subject the last time. She was going to tell Dawn Kendall—in her own good time. But she certainly didn't want it coming from Cameron.

'Be sensible, Nadine.' His mouth was a hard line of determination now. 'What are you going to do? Leave it until it shows? She isn't that stupid that she won't realise it for herself—and pretty soon by the way that waistline of yours is expanding.'

'All right!' She took a deep breath as she sat forward in her seat, gritting her teeth. 'But you can't just go telling her it's yours!'

'Why on earth not?' She felt the glare of his eyes even though her gaze was fixed on the number-plate of the car in front. 'What exactly are you planning to tell her? "I'm having a baby but I don't know who the father is"?' His anger had risen swiftly, so that it was almost palpable. 'I won't let you discredit our child's origins like that—any more than I would deny fathering it myself!'

'You'll have to!' Panic filled her voice now.

'*Oh*, no!'

Of course. He would adhere to the truth—and his responsibility—whatever the consequences.

'I won't make you divulge the actual terms that led to our baby's conception—but there's no way I'll ever let you tell anyone that that child isn't mine!'

Nadine swallowed hard, biting her lower lip, trying to avoid looking into the rear-view mirror. 'She'll think...everyone will think I had an affair with you,' she said in a small pained whisper.

Suddenly, from behind, the other car overtook her on the left, its horn hooting loudly.

'That will be the inevitable deduction—yes,' he said resignedly. But he didn't care because it wasn't the truth, and he wasn't a man to worry about what people thought. 'It's either that—or tell her the truth.' Coolly now, he acquainted her with the hard, bare facts. 'And I'm sure you'd agree the former will be the lesser of two evils.'

He was right, of course. If she told anyone she'd conceived his child purely for money they'd think the worst about her—as he had, she thought with a small, ironic twist to her lips. That she was nothing but a mercenary little gold-digger. And if she told the truth, her mother would probably die of grief.

'All right,' she said again, but defeatedly this time. 'Only she isn't very strong at the moment. Let me tell her. It's my place to, and I know I should have done it before now.'

So that was it. The worst was over, Nadine thought, sitting beside the bed where Dawn Kendall had retired to take a couple of hours' rest before they had come in. And it had been made surprisingly easier because Cameron had insisted on being there, and also because when she'd written to her mother about Lisa's accident some weeks ago something had impelled Nadine to relate that her friend and Cameron had split up.

'Why didn't you tell me?' The woman had looked shocked at first, and she'd cried a little, so that it had wrung Nadine's heart having to cause her mother such inevitable distress.

She'd wanted to say, Because you were so ill, but she didn't, because she knew how reluctant her mother was to acknowledge it. So all she said softly was, 'You know why.'

'No, Nadine didn't tell me, Mrs Kendall.' Cameron, standing on the other side of the bed, reassured her softly in response to the questioning glance she had sent his way. 'I'm afraid I stumbled upon the knowledge that you were unwell quite by accident, and not through Nadine breaking any promise she might have made to you. I'm also sorry this had to be sprung on you like this, and I'm quite aware of how things must look. But Lisa and I were already in deep water before any of this took place, and I'd like you to rest assured that the breakup of my marriage had nothing at all to do with the way I felt about Nadine.'

How coolly he could say it! And so easily because it was true, she thought with a stabbing anguish across her heart. He felt nothing for her! And listening to him placating her mother with that strong, charismatic personality, she saw Dawn Kendall visibly softening—melting beneath that irresistible masculine charm.

'I also think you should know, Mrs Kendall, that it is my firm intention to marry Nadine before the baby's born.'

Nadine looked at him quickly, utterly taken aback, but that cool masculine gaze didn't falter, only diverted smilingly to the woman who had caught his hand along with Nadine's.

'You really have been keeping a lot from me, haven't you?' Softly the woman chided her daughter, but she was smiling too, and through a riveting numbness Nadine could see tears glistening in her mother's eyes.

How dared he? Indignation had replaced her numbness by the time he followed her downstairs, and in the sitting-room, out of earshot, she turned on him with angry colour in her cheeks.

'Just who do you think you are—leading Mum to think we're going to get married?' she castigated fiercely. Now she'd only be hurt and disappointed when she realised it wasn't true. 'Why did you have to tell her that?'

'Because we are.'

His very decisive response had her mouth dropping open in shock before she recovered herself enough to utter tremulously, 'And don't you think I have a right to say something on the subject?'

He slipped a hand into his trouser pocket, infuriatingly composed in comparison. 'If you've any concern at all for our child, you'll say yes.'

'Of course I care about it! But that's not the point!' Nadine breathed, dumbfounded. How could she agree to marry him—live with him—knowing he didn't love her; knowing for ever afterwards that he'd only proposed to her out of duty? She couldn't! 'I don't want to marry you.' It caused a tearing sensation inside of her to say it. 'Give me one good reason why I should.'

'One good...?' His expression was hard and disbelieving. 'I would have thought the baby was reason enough!' he flung incredulously at her.

Of course. He would say that. Because he didn't share her fears, the bitter memories of her own childhood that still clawed into her like vicious talons. 'No. I don't want to,' she reiterated flatly, her features taut with resolve.

'Why not?' He was advancing towards her, his stature hard and imposing. 'Because you're anti-men?'

So he still believed that about her.

'I—I can't,' she uttered, swallowing, and then, more tentatively, 'I—I don't love you.' But she couldn't look at him as she said it, and wondered if she imagined that rasp of breath through his lungs.

'It's all what *you* want, isn't it?' he said savagely, pulling her to face him. 'Well, I don't give a damn what you feel about me. The child's my only concern, and I don't want it being born illegitimate now that it doesn't have to be.'

His fingers bit into her shoulders, making her wince, and looking up at him emphatically she murmured, 'Surely it doesn't matter these days? Illegitimacy's no longer a stigma, and a lot of children do better with single parents than with two who are constantly involved in bitter quarrels. I know. I certainly would have.'

'Possibly,' he acceded, 'but our child won't be one of them. If I start beating you then you can divorce me, but I don't think that's very likely. And any marriage of ours would probably stand a better chance of succeeding than the one in three that fail,' he assured her with a sudden grim cast to his features. 'After all, it's hardly going to be complicated by love, is it?'

He couldn't have hurt her more if he'd used the physical violence he'd flippantly referred to, and she glanced down at the fine cotton of his shirt so that he wouldn't see the wounded emotion in her eyes.

'You know you want me, Nadine.' His voice had turned insidiously soft. 'At least we have that much in common.' That killingly seductive tone, with the light touch of his fingers under her chin, stripped away any resistance she might have had against the mouth that was clamping possessively over hers.

His kiss was shatteringly suggestive, the deep probing of his tongue in the moist recesses of her mouth making her ache for a more fulfilling intimacy. But then her surfacing instincts of self-preservation had her struggling against it, resisting the steel-hard strength of those arms around her, so that almost reluctantly, it seemed, he lifted his head.

'Think it over,' he said impassively, those thick black lashes lowered, concealing any emotion as he released her to cross over to the phone to ring for his taxi. 'I'm sure you'll agree that it's the best solution all round.'

The first nip was in the air the day she moved back into the cottage, three weeks later, and Tuesday showed every sign of being pleased to see her, having arrived with Edna who had already aired and cleaned the place from top to bottom.

'Well, you don't want to go doing too much,' was her solicitous comment when Nadine told her she shouldn't have gone to so much trouble. 'Not now.' She beamed, that last meaningful remark assuring Nadine that Edna had guessed. 'I've got three of me own. I'd be blind if I hadn't recognised the signs,' she admitted, in response to Nadine's silently surprised query. 'I can tell you, though, it's about the only way you can get a man to pamper you—so I'd make the most of it, if I were you!'

Nadine laughed, relaxing. Of course Edna would realise. A man wouldn't be spending as much time with his young and pregnant tenant as Cameron was spending down here if he wasn't very probably the baby's father. She also knew that Edna wouldn't gossip about her or Cameron to anyone else.

He came down that weekend, helping Nadine pick up the last of the apples in the orchard that had fallen during a particularly windy few days.

'You know, we could make this our regular weekend home if you wanted to,' he said as they came through into the homely kitchen, which still smelt of the bread she'd baked earlier. 'We could extend this room into the garden if you think it could do with expanding a little. Just agree to marry me and I'll get the work started right away.'

Nadine tensed, dumping the last bag of apples down on to the table with all the others beside the jars of cooling jam she'd been making with the ripe plums she had frozen the previous month. 'Cameron, I've already told you—— Oooh!'

A strange sensation in her tummy had her suddenly clutching her middle.

'What is it?'

He looked worried, immensely so, and a small bubble of laughter burst from her lips. 'It moved,' she breathed, unable to conceal her wonderment. 'The baby. It moved. My tummy's felt as though it's been rumbling all day, but it's the baby!'

The hard lines of his face seemed to soften as he came around the table, and with an arm around her shoulders he laid his other hand lightly on her middle. His fingers were strong, yet gentle at the same time, their light caress sending little tingles of pleasure shivering through her.

'It isn't doing it now.' Her voice shook from a whole sphere of bewildering emotions, her breath catching as Cameron bent his head and gently kissed her mouth.

'Then we'll just have to stay here until it does,' he murmured teasingly against her lips.

The chemistry between them, however, was too sensually charged for either of them to indulge in such light-hearted games, and suddenly he was pushing her back on to the hard pine of the table, sending ripe fruit rolling off the edge on to the floor.

Her hands clutching his shoulders, Nadine drew him down to her, accepting the hard domination of his weight on hers, his superior strength, the devouring intensity of his mouth.

She murmured her acquiescence as his lips slid down her throat, giving a shuddering gasp when he pushed back her blouse and the lace of her bra to caress gently the rounded fullness of her breast, thinking she would die of pleasure when his mouth found the taut, warm crest his hand had manipulated into arousal.

'Oh, God! You're as sweet a harvest as any man could wish for,' he groaned against her breast, his hands sliding over the ripening contours of her body. But when she lifted her hips in sensuous provocation against his, unable to contain the surge of raw need that racked her, he pulled away from her, saying firmly, 'No. I'm not grabbing snatched pleasures with you like some visiting country squire with his latest kitchen-maid. When we make love again it's got to be in the right place—in our own bed—as a respectable married couple.'

With a whimper of frustration, Nadine closed her eyes, trying to shut out the image his words conjured up. How wonderful it sounded! she thought. But such physical pleasure needed love to make it worthwhile, and while she had all the feeling for him she could hold to make a commitment like that work on her side, she knew there was none on his.

'There's no way I'm going to marry you, Cameron,' she murmured, with drawn down lashes hiding dark, tortured eyes as she sat up, gasping when his hand slid possessively over her breast before she could pull her blouse together.

He laughed, and though she wasn't looking at him she could see that eyebrow lifting, mocking that involuntary response. 'No?'

'No,' she said tenaciously, but with a shiver of apprehension too, because she could feel the net of his determination tightening, the building pressure on her to do the right thing. Surely, though, it wasn't right to allow her child to be born into a loveless marriage—was it?

she wondered harrowingly. And surely Cameron couldn't insist on it if she objected? Of course he couldn't, she thought, telling herself not to be so foolish.

But the questions remained to worry her, not only then, but every succeeding day as the baby continued to grow.

Another source of pressure came, albeit unintentionally, from Dawn Kendall. The prospect of her forthcoming grandchild had seemed somehow to speed her recovery, giving her something to look ahead to, and Nadine knew her mother was also looking forward to seeing her daughter married.

'The last thing I expected was to be a grandmother,' the woman enthused the next time Nadine was in London visiting her. 'But I'll be happier when I can say I've got a son-in-law as well.'

Nadine laughed awkwardly, quickly changing the subject. How could she tell her mother she wasn't going to marry Cameron? she thought, annoyed with him for building up the woman's hopes in the way he had. Because if she told her that, she'd have to explain why— that he didn't really love her—and then she'd have to reveal her deepest fears, and there was no way that she wanted to do that.

'Just concentrate on continuing to get fit,' she advised amiably, as she left to drive into town.

But the increasing pressure on her to marry Cameron— from Cameron himself, her mother, and her own desire to do what was best for the baby—was making her irritable and edgy, so that she had to pull herself up from getting unduly impatient with a few rather incautious drivers during her journey.

For the same reason her mind was preoccupied as, having finished her shopping, she turned into a busy Regent Street and, not looking where she was going, collided embarrassingly with someone.

'Nadine!'

'Larry?' She scarcely recognised him. His hair was long now and secured in a ponytail, and his sweater and torn jeans bore the distinct look of a man in voluntary distress.

Cameron was right, she thought grudgingly. Larry had revolted against all his father's principles and conservative society. But it was great to see him again, and so she leaped at the opportunity of a long chat with him when he said, 'You aren't in a hurry, are you? Do you fancy a coffee?'

In a small café just off noisy Regent Street, Larry told her what he'd been doing. 'I'm painting these days— pictures, not houses!' he laughed. 'Although a few of us have got an old barn that we're renovating. I don't suppose it would be any use asking you if you'd like to join us?'

In a commune? Nadine grimaced to herself, but with a hand on her heart said laughingly, 'I'd love to—but I'm allergic to decorating!'

'I thought it might be too much to expect.' He winked at her and she knew a warming pleasure from the repartee she had always shared with him. 'I suppose you think, like everyone else, that I'm throwing away my chances and my education,' he said on a more serious note. 'But I had to get out of the rat-race. It really wasn't for me. I'm sorry I left as I did—without a word—but I was too mixed up to contact anybody at the time. What have you been doing, anyway? If you don't mind me saying so, you've put on a bit of weight, and I like it. It suits you.'

Nadine laughed. 'Have I?' Dear Larry. He hadn't realised yet. 'I must have been eating too many Sally Lunns,' she giggled.

'Sorry?' From the look he gave her he obviously wasn't sure what she was talking about, and she dismissed it with a smile. 'You haven't changed in one respect, though.' Amused, he glanced down at the little china teapot she was carefully draining. 'I've still never known anyone drink so much tea!'

She laughed again. 'My mother's always said I've got hollow legs,' she admitted, feeling happier than she had felt in weeks. It was great to pretend that everything was the same as it had been before she had become pregnant, to forget—if only for a little while—the dilemma that had been weighing her down since Cameron had proposed.

'Do you see anyone from the old firm?' Larry wanted to know when she told him very broadly that she was now living and working away from London. She shook her head.

'I forgot what a private person you are. How you never allowed anyone to get that close to you. Including me,' Larry emphasised with a feigned disapproval that made her smile.

No, she hadn't forged many close relationships in her life, she realised suddenly—beyond a few casual friends. Only with Lisa. And Cameron, she thought poignantly. And look where those had got her.

'I've got to go!' The rush-hour was building up and she'd arranged to meet Cameron at his office. 'I've really got to dash,' she said when they were out on the busy street. 'It's been lovely seeing you again.'

'Yes, it has,' Larry agreed absently above the noise of the traffic, because he was frowning down at the lengthy sweater she was wearing over her skirt, and suddenly he said, 'For heaven's sake, kick me in the teeth if I'm stepping out of line, but... are you pregnant?'

She laughed at the surprised embarrassment on his face, and on impulse reached up to plant a light kiss on his cheek.

'It's all that tea. My legs filled up and it had nowhere else to go,' she jested. 'But you're bang on target. And, no—I'm not telling you anything about it now.'

He wanted to ask. She could see the curiosity burning in his eyes. But he respected her privacy too much to press the point, completely throwing her off-guard as his unconcealed delight urged him into grabbing her and kissing her full on the lips.

She was still laughing as she watched him lope off into the crowd, and turning round, her face all smiles, walked straight into Cameron.

CHAPTER SEVEN

'WELL, well. So this is what you meant when you said you'd be visiting your mother?' Cameron's tone was as chilling as the cold hostility with which he was regarding her. 'No wonder you made some excuse about not being up here in time to have lunch with me. You were too busy meeting that no-hoper of a drop-out, Lawson!'

'That's not true!'

'Isn't it?'

'No! I did see Mum,' she shouted above the deafening drone of a pneumatic drill that had suddenly started up across the street. And, as it burred into merciful silence, 'I just didn't think it would be fair to cut my visit short by leaving so soon.'

Cameron's mouth twisted with hard scepticism. 'But you had no qualms about meeting Larry as soon as your duty was executed.'

'I didn't *meet* him—as you put it! And don't refer to my seeing my mother as a duty!' she flung at him woundedly as the drill started up again, although she could tell from the way his jaw clenched that he'd instantly regretted making that remark.

'Are you in love with him?' he demanded, his fingers bruising on her arm as he dragged her close enough to make himself heard. 'Is that why you were kissing him?'

'I wasn't kissing him. He was kissing *me*!' she threw back, wishing they were anywhere but there in the heart of a noisy West End that was nearing its rush-hour.

'What's the difference?' he said harshly. 'Whichever way round—you appeared to be enjoying it!'

'Oh, sure! I get my kicks out of being pregnant and fooling around with other men!'

116

'That's what it looks like!' He was shouting too, and she couldn't bear it. She loved him too much to have this sort of heated row with him.

'Well, to you it would!' she screamed, her throat hurting, her voice growing hoarse from trying to make herself heard above the burr of that infernal drill. 'If I didn't know you were such a pig-headed brute I'd have said you were jealous...!'

She hadn't intended to say that, and instantly she clammed up, staring questioningly up at him. Were his feelings that obvious? Did he *care* about her? Or was it just his shattered male ego from seeing her in the arms of another man that was making him look as though he wanted to kill her?

'Just don't say anything else,' he warned through gritted teeth, and still clasping her roughly by the arm hailed an approaching taxi. 'We'll settle this in private without letting the whole of the West End in on our affairs!'

And 'private' meant the superb London home he had shared with Lisa, Nadine realised, hearing him issuing instructions to the driver before a tense and silent journey brought them to the luxurious Georgian terrace.

'Now,' he breathed, slamming the front door closed behind them, his footsteps echoing ominously after hers across the marble floor, 'you'd better start explaining what you think you're doing carrying on with that... that——' He was gesturing roughly back at the door, as though the invisible Larry was standing behind him. 'That brainless rebel!'

'I wasn't carrying on with him! And he isn't brainless!' Nadine shouted, in defence of her old boss.

'That's debatable!' His voice was rising too, a vein in his neck pulsing hard above the crisp whiteness of his collar. 'How easily you defend him, Nadine. Would you care to explain to me why?' His voice was smoother now, harshly controlled. 'Isn't it because your relationship with him was a lot more than just professional? Isn't that why you were kissing him?'

'I told you. I wasn't! He was kissing *me*!'

'What's the difference?' He laughed humourlessly. 'As I said, you appeared to be enjoying it!'

'That's right! I did!' she snapped back when she could see he wasn't going to listen to reason. 'And why shouldn't I? You don't own me!' She heard him coming after her as she swept away from him, into the elegantly furnished sitting-room. 'I've got a right to kiss anybody I like—whoever, whenever and *wherever* I please!'

'Not while you're pregnant with my child, you haven't!' he said savagely. And then suddenly, brutally, 'If you weren't it would be a totally different matter.'

So that was all he cared about. For a while she had been hoping that there might have been a flicker of jealousy in him; just one glimmer that might have given her a ray of hope that he cared about her for herself, if only a little. But there was none. His heart was as devoid of love for her as the luxurious room was of its familiarly feminine touches—of Lisa's mark upon it. Absently her tortured gaze digested it. It was as though he'd stripped it of every vestige of her presence, with only the modern furniture and wall-covering she'd chosen remaining. With a searing pain across her heart Nadine wondered if perhaps, beneath that obvious bitterness about his marriage, it hurt too much to remember.

Oh, God! Her hands came to rest on the mantelpiece, fingers curling tensely into the hard white marble as she strove for equilibrium. She could never marry him as he wanted her to do, knowing she'd always be such a poor substitute for Lisa.

'The baby's all you think about, isn't it?' She had to stifle a sob as she met his inexorable features in the mirror hanging above the fireplace, every familiar curve of his arrogant bone-structure, his leanness, his confident stance, making her heart twist from the inner struggle not to forget all her reservations and marry him. But unintentionally, she realised, he had just offered her a way out.

Strained from the effort it was taking to accept it, and through a suffocating anguish, she was reiterating impetuously, 'It's all you care about—and not for its own sake but because you're so screwed up about what life did to you! But what makes you so bloody certain it's yours?'

For a moment a frown creased that high, tanned forehead in the mirror. The next he was uttering a curt, harsh laugh.

'Oh, come on, Nadine! We both know that when I took you initially I was the first. So you can dispense with those little feminine contrivances to shock me— and that unbecoming language.' His tone conveyed what she already knew. He hated women swearing. 'You were a virgin.' He seemed to take great satisfaction in reminding her.

'Yes.' Her futile love for him drove her on. 'But not the morning after!' she declared tremulously, pivoting round to meet the hard, deepening question in his eyes.

'Just what are you getting at?' he whispered, his face taut and ashen, bloodlessly cold.

Nadine swallowed, hating herself, but she had to pursue this course, and not just for her own sake, she convinced herself, but for everyone's. 'You're being rather slow, Cameron. After that wonderful initiation, what reason was there for holding out any longer? You and Lisa wanted a baby—I wanted the money. And two chances of getting pregnant were twice as good as one!' After all, he'd as good as accused her of it that day he'd telephoned the flat!

She uttered a small, frightened cry as he lifted his arm, and what strength of will it took for him to refrain from striking her she never knew, seeing only the white rage in his face as his hand twisted cruelly in her thick red hair instead, tugging her head back, his angry strength forcing her hard against the mantelpiece.

'You little whore!' His savage whisper made her realise shamefully how far she had gone.

'I'm not!' It was a desperate attempt to absolve herself from the indiscriminate things she had wanted him to believe about her. He was looking at her as though he hated her and she couldn't bear it; that frighteningly controlled reaction from him was causing her real fear. 'It wasn't true! None of it was true! Please, Cameron, you're hurting me. I promise! None of it was true!'

'No?' His mouth was cruelly derisive as he regarded her proud yet tortured features. 'It would have been a real plan of duplicity—sleeping with one man for enough cash to set yourself up with another who wasn't too inclined to work. Wouldn't it?' Was that what he believed? 'But no. As cosy and convenient an arrangement as that might have been, I know you well enough by now, dearest, to realise that even you aren't that morally corrupt. The real truth is that you'd say anything—do anything—if you thought it would let you off the hook and get me out of your life. Isn't that it, Nadine? Isn't this all one last childish endeavour to avoid the unavoidable—avoid doing what you know to be right?'

His capacity for reading her mind never ceased to astonish her, but she held her guarded eyes level with his to murmur calmly, 'Marrying you would never be right.'

Some deep, personal emotion made him draw in a breath. Was he thinking the same thing? Here in this house, where he had lived and loved with Lisa? Striving to stifle the love beneath the rigid self-discipline of duty?

She couldn't look at him as he turned her towards him, afraid of revealing the emotion she knew would show in her eyes.

'I didn't want to have to take a hard line with you, Nadine,' she heard him whisper inexorably above her, 'but I'm afraid you leave me no choice. If you refuse to put the child first—help me provide it with a secure and stable future—then I warn you now, as much as I applaud your reasons behind your conceiving the baby in the first place, I'll fight you tooth and nail to make sure it gets the right chance in life. I'll fight—even if it takes until doomsday for me to get absolute care and control.'

'You wouldn't win!' Panic tautened her features, distant memory stirring that cold, indissoluble fear. 'You admitted that yourself, months ago. Surrogate mothers aren't legally bound to give up their babies if they decide not to——'

'Not usually, no,' he accepted, with a phlegmatism that scared her. 'But there have been exceptions. And our child's conception differs immensely from the usual artificial methods that most surrogacy arrangements utilise. We've had a relationship, Nadine. That puts me in a far stronger position with regard to my rights over the child. And, win or lose, I hardly think it's fair to subject your mother not only to the obvious kind of distress a battle like that between us might cause, but to finding out why her grandchild was really conceived. Because as much as I understand your wanting to keep the facts from her, they're bound to come out, Nadine. I can't prevent that.'

'You'd really go ahead?' she whispered numbly. 'Knowing what it might do to her?' He didn't answer, the determined set to his mouth all the confirmation she needed. 'You unscrupulous louse!' Tears brightening her eyes, she hated him in that moment with all the strength of the counterbalancing side of her love for him. 'You really know how to play on a person's weaknesses, don't you? And what makes you think you'd be in a stronger position to sue for custody than I would? You'd still be a single parent.'

'Except that I'd be prepared to marry—for the sake of my child.'

He meant someone else, and the realisation of it caused her chest to tighten in anguish, along with the unthinkable possibility of her baby going to another woman. And the influence he might be able to exert because of his own standing with the courts...

'You've got all the answers, haven't you?' she breathed tremulously. 'Those poor devils who come up against you in court really haven't got a chance, have they?'

He shrugged, and she caught the glint of some emotion beneath those heavy lids, though she couldn't tell what it was. 'Only if they've got a strong enough case to withstand the pressure.'

'Which I don't have?'

'You know you haven't.'

Her expression that of one already beaten, she sent him a glance from beneath her lashes, wondering what he would do if she called his bluff. She wasn't certain whether he would carry out his threat, but she couldn't take that chance. The scars of his own illegitimacy were too deeply etched for him to see his own child suffer in the same way, and he would go to any lengths—even sacrificing his own happiness—and hers—to see that it didn't happen.

'You're despicable,' she breathed, her shoulders sagging.

A brief glimmer of satisfaction touched his lips in recognising her statement for exactly what it was—defeat—but then it was gone, and something dark and tumultuous clouded the blue depths of his eyes.

'Why don't you just say you hate me?' he advised tonelessly. 'After all, that's what you mean, isn't it?'

A tremor shivered through Nadine, his nearness weakening her so that she had to struggle to respond evenly, achingly, 'If you know, why ask?'

Some inner conflict gripped him. Pride, she thought, as she felt his fingers tense on her upper arms, saw that hard, lean look about him that gave him the appearance of a hunted jungle animal. But dispassionately he smiled and said, 'Sometimes hate can be as strong an aphrodisiac as love.' And then he was claiming her mouth in a kiss of such determined possession that for a moment she couldn't breathe, couldn't think, couldn't feel anything but the dominating power of his body against hers, his hard, exciting strength. 'At least we have this in common,' he stated when even her silent refusal to respond failed to negate the tense arousal of her body. 'So why don't we make it a marriage we can both enjoy instead of a situation which one of us feels we're entering on sufferance?'

Her voice was bitter as she pulled out of his grasp. 'And give you victory all round?'

'Is that how you see it?' he rasped, and against the flush of desire in his face his eyes shone like glittering blue steel.

No, I see myself loving you—and you never, ever loving me! her mind cried torturedly in response. But she couldn't tell him that, and when she didn't answer she thought she heard him utter under his breath, 'Then so be it.'

They were married at a register office three weeks later, with only Simon Braith and his fiancée and Dawn Kendall in attendance.

In a cream jersey dress and three-quarter-length jacket, the loose lines of which helped cloak if not altogether conceal the fact that she was pregnant, Nadine stood like a beautiful pale statue, with her hair swept elegantly off her face, posing for photographs with Cameron in the cold November sunshine. As the cheery little man called laughingly to them, 'Right! That should be enough to show your grandchildren!' she wondered, through a little cloud of anxiety, if Cameron's lack of love for her could sustain their marriage throughout their child's upbringing, let alone into a second generation.

And uncannily, reading her thoughts as he so often did, he said, 'What's wrong, Nadine? Can't you imagine yourself old and grey with me?' Then, with amusement turning to something harder and more cynical, 'Or are you regretting making a lifelong commitment to me already?'

That note of detachment in his voice sent an almost discernible shudder through her, and the sudden, crushing intensity of his embrace demonstrated possession rather than any real affection for her as he kissed her long and fully on the mouth.

An affected little cough finally forced him into releasing her, bringing her teetering senses to the beautiful brunette who was uttering sultrily, 'Steady on, Cam.' It was the young woman she had seen at Lisa's funeral, who now was looking at her with a kind of mocking condescension, as though she knew just how shaken she was from the shattering thoroughness of that kiss. 'It's not every woman, you know, who enjoys such demonstrative mastery in public.'

From that remark Nadine gathered—as she felt she was supposed to—that this woman had experienced the same slaying surrender—and with Cameron, she thought, piqued. She was relieved to realise that no one else had been watching. The photographer was already putting his tripod into the back of his estate car and Dawn—looking better than she had in years, if still a little thin, in her classic green suit and hat, Nadine decided—was listening to something Molly was saying, while Simon listened indulgently at her side.

'Rachael.' With impeccable courtesy Cameron acknowledged the newcomer, introducing her to Nadine as Rachael Hampshire, Lisa's second cousin. But did it not bother him, having a relative of Lisa's at his wedding? Nadine couldn't help wondering. Or did that urbane smile hide a barely concealed annoyance? She wasn't sure.

'I must say you look lovely,' Rachael announced rather effusively to Nadine, though the girl's svelte image, created by a tailored red suit and sleek raven hair that cascaded from a middle parting like an advert for some shampoo, gave her a chicness which, at five and a half months pregnant, Nadine was aware she sorely lacked.

'I didn't expect to see you here, Rachael.' Again, Nadine sensed that tight restraint behind Cameron's smile.

'I know you didn't ask me, Cam,' the girl returned with smiling admonishment, 'but I thought you'd need some familial support on a special day like this. Did you think I'd be too upset? Or perhaps wouldn't understand so soon aft——'

Whether it was the hard look on Cameron's face or her own integrity that had stopped her actually saying what she had been going too, Nadine couldn't decide; she was only aware that Rachael had checked herself—and quickly—before going on to say, 'You shouldn't have kept it such a quiet affair. No one would have expected anything else...' Cursorily, her gaze flitted over Nadine's burgeoning figure. 'In the circumstances.'

'It isn't anyone else's affair.' Cameron's response came back like gun-fire, hard and aggressive. But why? Nadine wondered achingly. Because it tortured him so much putting duty above the love he still felt for Lisa?

'Of course it isn't.' Rachael gave a sexy little laugh, oozing charm—a charm which would be irresistible to men, Nadine recognised, experiencing a swift, hot resentment as the girl reached up to kiss Cameron lightly on the mouth.

'You don't mind, do you?' The brown eyes fixed on Nadine were almost convincing in their apology, but there was desolation too, in their translucent depths, an emptiness as acute as her own.

'Of course not.' So why was she seething inside? Was it because Rachael Hampshire was so stunningly attractive—and so slim in contrast? Nadine thought disconsolately, wondering what Cameron had told this girl about her and the baby. She was glad of the diversion from her unsettlingly thoughts as Simon strolled across and with gentlemanly courtesy asked if he might kiss the bride.

His question was directed at Cameron, and her husband's laughingly possessive, 'That's quite enough Simon!' when the other man kissed her on the cheek, made her heart ache at how easily he could pretend to be the besotted groom.

Holding her away from him, the tall, fair-haired man said quietly, 'Make him happy, Nadine.'

She frowned, noting the depth of feeling in his voice. But then Dawn and Molly were coming over to add their congratulations, sweeping everything else out of her mind. Everything save for Cameron talking intimately with Rachael before the wedding-car drew up to whisk bride and groom away.

Their honeymoon was a warm, lazy ten days in the Canary Islands, and a welcome break from the dreary cold of a British November. Ten days when Nadine almost forgot that her marriage was simply a marriage of necessity, because Cameron, she found, could be not only surprisingly romantic, but fun.

'You danced me off my feet last night!' she protested, waking one morning to find him already dressed and ready to go swimming, urging her to get up.

'Not quite. I'm saving that until there's only one of you. Anyway, I thought I got you to bed early enough.' His sensual teasing brought back the vivid reminder of the passionate hours she had spent in his arms afterwards, unable, as she had been from the start, to deny herself the devastating ecstasy of his lovemaking. In that way, she'd been proved too weak. 'Now, are you going to get up—or am I going to have to——?'

'All right!' Realising his intention to subject her feet to a merciless tickling, she jumped, shrieking, out of bed. 'You won't leave me alone for a minute, will you?' she remonstrated, unable to help laughing as she said it, fun turning to that familiar heightened awareness of him as he grabbed her as she was fastening her robe, catching her possessively to him.

'That's something I promise never to do,' he breathed against her lips, the pledge so sensual as he took command of her mouth that desire whipped through her like a ravaging storm, tempered only by the knowledge that while hers was fed by love his was triggered by nothing more than a healthy masculine urge. 'Now, go and get your swimsuit on before we wind up in bed again.

I've no objection, but other kinds of exercise are important for you too, Mrs Hunter.'

So they swam, and dined by candlelight, and walked hand in hand along the moonlit beach. They were assuming a façade of being happy because circumstances had forced them together, Nadine thought, watching him swim from the shore. Each act was a prelude—a mere softening—for the one thing that required no pretence or false emotion on either of their parts, she thought ruefully, unable to deny the piercing desire in her loins as she thought about their shattering compatibility in bed.

When they returned to London, they were already into December, and before Nadine realised it, Christmas was upon them.

Dawn Kendall came to stay for the holiday which, to Nadine's relief, Cameron suggested they spend at the cottage. His insistence that she put her own flat on the market and they live in what, after all, had been Lisa's London home, wasn't something she'd been happy about, although she hadn't expressed as much openly to him. At the cottage, though, there was nothing to remind her of the happy times he must have shared with Lisa— to make her feel that she was an intruder in another woman's house. Christmas, therefore, was particularly enjoyable, especially as Dawn stayed almost until the New Year.

'Don't wait up,' Cameron instructed Nadine firmly the night he was driving her mother back, causing Dawn to pull a face at her daughter as he went out to start the car.

'He certainly takes a governing hand with you, doesn't he?' she commented, expressing wry approval of her new son-in-law.

'He tries.' Nadine grimaced amiably, knowing that it would be alien to her husband's character to be anything but in command. 'But he doesn't always succeed.'

'Now, you should listen to him.' Her mother wagged a friendly scolding finger at her daughter. 'Especially over things that concern your physical health. For a start, he's a lot older than you are—and a lot more experienced. I'm far happier about you settling down with him than if you'd married a boy of your own age.'

'You make me sound like a child!' Nadine laughed. 'I didn't realise you wanted me to have a surrogate father!'

'He's got more control over you than your father had, my girl,' her mother assured her wisely, unwittingly reminding Nadine of the lack of responsibility her father had shown towards her rather than of any extreme wilfulness on her own part. 'And he's far from being a father-figure.'

'Just a bully!' Nadine supplied flippantly. She was watching Tuesday playing with one of the little glass balls hanging from the Christmas tree by the window, and against the little tinkle of bells she heard Dawn click her tongue disapprovingly.

'He knows the difference between bullying and straightforward firmness, and you should recognise it too. Anyone can see how important you are to him, with all the care and protection he lavishes on you.'

Only because he's concerned about the baby, Nadine sighed inwardly in response, although she didn't say it. She didn't want her mother to realise that she wasn't totally happy, that her marriage wasn't everything it seemed. Also, Dawn Kendall belonged to an era when women had believed that a man's word was law—which was probably why she had had such a hard time in her own marriage, Nadine thought sadly, determined she wouldn't be as subservient as her mother had been to any man.

When she and Cameron had gone, though, she missed them both considerably, turning the heating up, as the night had grown windy and particularly cold, and absorbing herself in the Christmas special of a recently finished television series, while Tuesday jumped up and nestled in for warmth against the maternal bulge of her middle.

Ignoring Cameron's order, she waited up. Half in defiance, she decided afterwards, because of the things her mother had said. Deep down, though, there were other, more important reasons for wanting to see him safely back at the cottage. But finding herself falling asleep while sewing ribbons on the little bootees her mother had made for the baby over the holiday, she decided to do the sensible thing and, finally submitting to Cameron's advice, took herself off to bed.

Once there, though, she found it almost impossible to sleep. Inside her the baby seemed to be practising for the Premier League, kicking away, as it often did, the instant she settled down. Nor did it help, as she laid a fondling hand over the active mound of her middle, to be thinking about its father, craving him in a fever of need only heightened by her condition, which gradually changed to one of anxiety as the night progressed and he still didn't come home.

Where was he? Why hadn't he come back yet? Was everything all right?

Worriedly the questions buzzed around her brain until, miraculously, somehow she drifted off to sleep.

When she awoke, she could see instantly that Cameron's side of the bed hadn't been slept in. The house seemed unduly quiet, and anxiously she slipped out of bed.

The night had brought a heavy fall of snow, she was surprised to discover when she pulled back the curtains, but just as she'd feared, Cameron's car wasn't outside. There were footprints in the deep snow leading to the front door. The milkman's or the postman's, she guessed, marvelling at how they had got through. But where was Cameron? Why hadn't he rung?

Really worried now, she picked up the bedside phone to telephone her mother, only to find the line was dead. The heavy snow must have brought the wires down, she thought uneasily, wondering what she should do next.

And then she heard it. The slow scrape of metal on stone somewhere outside.

With anticipation leaping through her, she pulled on warm trousers and a thick sweater and went downstairs to investigate, gasping with pure relief as she opened the kitchen door.

Similarly attired, Cameron was clearing snow from the path at the back of the house, so preoccupied that he didn't notice her immediately, which gave her time to pull her features into more neutral lines.

'Good morning.' The crooked smile he gave her tugged at her heartstrings as he suddenly glanced up and saw her. 'Welcome to the North Pole.'

'And I suppose you're Santa Claus!' she gibed, her tone cynical from the anxieties she had been nursing about him. 'I didn't see your car outside. I didn't think you'd come home.'

'I didn't.' The spade he was wielding scraped loudly on the path as he shovelled snow into a heap on one side. 'Not last night anyway. The blizzard was so bad by the time I reached Bath, I decided to check in to a hotel. I tried to ring you but the line was dead. The main roads have been cleared but the side roads are treacherous, and this lane's impassable. I had to abandon the car in the village and walk up.'

'I was worried about you.' Damn! Why did she have to say that? Now he'd guess at the agonies she'd suffered thinking something had happened to him, she berated herself, seeing the quizzical emotion that tilted the corners of his mouth.

'Have no fear. I don't intend on making you a widow just yet,' he assured her drily. 'But if it means I'm missed, I'll stay away more often. What would you have done if I hadn't got back? Sent an expedition out to look for me? Or counted your blessings that you'd been let off so easily?'

He might have been joking, but there was no laughter in his eyes. Rather, she sensed a vulnerability behind that capable strength that she wanted to reach out and touch, and yet it was as far away as the moon, she thought achingly, her heart crying, Think what you like, but if you died, I'd want to die too!

'You'll never know, will you?' she parried lightly instead, and shuddering inwardly from the startling depth of her emotions, flounced back inside to make some tea.

It was early in the afternoon that they decided to go for a walk. The sun had come out around lunchtime, turning an earlier grey sky to a rather watery blue, and muffled in anoraks, gloves and boots, and with Tuesday happily confined to the house, together they set out into the virgin snow.

'Be careful,' Cameron warned when she slipped as they were trudging across the meadow where the horses usually grazed, although there was no sign of them today. Only a thrush flew shrieking across the field, alarmed by their approach—the only sign of life, besides themselves, in the silent, wintry landscape. 'Give me your hand.' So why did such a simple gesture cause such an upheaval in her? 'You look tired.' Assiduously, his eyes searched her face. 'You didn't wait up last night?'

'No,' she returned, noting the smallest admonition in his voice. 'But I couldn't sleep.'

'Missing me again?'

A rush of colour deepened the winter-nipped pink of her cheeks. Of course he'd realise, she thought, and said adamantly, 'No, I was just cold.'

'That's what I mean,' he drawled.

'You would,' she upbraided wryly, although a traitorous acknowledgment of that mutual sexual chemistry throbbed deep inside her. 'Apart from that, the baby wouldn't keep still.'

He laughed. 'A sign that my offspring's definitely fit and healthy. Aren't pregnant women supposed to get up in the middle of the night and start decorating the house, or some such similar occupation? You could have tried counting sheep. They say it's a good sedative. Or maybe you could count the number of babies' names you've chosen and abandoned. Are you any nearer to making your mind up about that?'

'No.' She laughed at her own inability to decide. 'Anyway, I don't see you coming up with anything acceptable.'

He shrugged beneath the thick, dark anorak. 'I suppose it depends on what day it's born.'

'Why?' she asked, looking up at him frowningly.

His smile was white against the cold-induced ruddiness of his cheeks. 'We've already got a Tuesday.'

'You idiot!' She gave him a playful nudge with her hip. 'I suppose we could always name it after a month. We could try March. April. May.' She paused between each one, considering how it sounded. 'June. Ju——'

'Hey, hold on! Are you expecting something four-legged or just a twelve-month pregnancy? Anyway, none of those are any good.'

'Why not?' She laughed up at him, enjoying this ridiculous speculation with him.

'Because they're all girls' names and it's going to be a boy.'

'Oh, really?' In the wintry sun her eyes shone like summer pools, their green depths challenging. Her every cell was alive to his nearness, to his wonderful presence, to the feel of the cold supple leather of the gloves her mother had given him for Christmas. 'And what makes you so certain? It might be a girl, and what would you do then?'

'Send it back and ask for a refund. You're going to give me a boy—the girls can come later. But first and foremost a man needs an heir to carry on his name.'

'You chauvinistic——!' His deep laughter as she pulled away from him told her he was only teasing her. Nevertheless, she took great delight in scooping up a handful of snow into a tight ball and hurling it straight at him. He made to duck, but it hit him full on the temple, exploding in white powdery flakes all over his hair and his dark jacket.

'Oh, we're playing that game, are we?' he observed, amused, and there was an undertone of some exciting threat beneath the laughter echoing her own.

'No!' She didn't stand a chance of avoiding his retaliatory shot, which landed exactly where he had aimed it, and taken by surprise she brushed hectically at the dampening patch on the seat of her trousers.

'That's not fair! You can throw harder than I can!' she wailed in mock-protest, hastily manufacturing another icy missile which she pelted right into the middle of his chest.

'Are you going to keep this up?' His words were jerky as he only just dodged another pelting.

'Why not?' Nadine laughed, enjoying herself.

'I'll tell you why not!' she heard him call back across the distance she was taking care to keep between them as she stooped to scoop up more snow. 'I can not only hit harder—I can run faster too!'

She gave a wild shriek as she saw him coming, but the snow was too deep for her to get away easily and she gave another little cry as he caught her. She was shrieking with amusement and the impetuous excitement that was racing through her as he turned her roughly in his arms, and the determination in his face induced her to submit to one last reckless urge and thrust a snowball beneath the thick polo-neck of his sweater.

'Right!' She twisted wildly in his grasp as he scooped snow from the laden branch of a tree and, grappling with the zipper of her anorak, showed every intention of doing the same thing to her.

'No, Cameron, don't! No, please! No!' The countryside rang with her shrieks as he tilted her back across his arm and, having loosened her jacket, was hell-bent on tugging at the sweater beneath.

'No, please, Cameron! No! Don't! I'm pregnant!'

'Really, Mrs Hunter, I'd never have guessed.' His breath rose with his deep laughter on the wintry air. She continued to scream her protests. 'All right. What's it worth?' he breathed with infuriating teasing, the face so close to hers alive with wicked intent.

A little frisson ran through her from the submissive pose in which he was holding her. 'A friendly wife?' she tossed up at him hotly, defying him to mete out the punishment she knew she richly deserved.

'Mmm... that sounds promising.'

'That isn't what I meant—and you know it!' she breathed, her heart pounding as he abandoned his threat and eased her upright without actually releasing her.

'Then let's see you stop me,' he drawled, dipping his head.

If she could have, she would have—if only for her pride's sake—but as his mouth covered hers all her longing—her need of him the previous night—surged through her with earth-rocking intensity.

Her arms came up around his neck as he locked her tightly to him, her response to his kiss flagrantly suggestive, her body straining to meet the overt demands of his.

She moaned her frustration as he separated them just for a moment to unfasten his own jacket, and then he was dragging her back to him, his mouth hungrier, his kiss more demanding than before.

The thick padding of his jacket was warm as she slipped her arms beneath it, aching to be closer to him, to feel the rousing heat of his body denied her by the inhibiting barrier of their clothes.

'Oh, God, Nadine, what you do to me!' he groaned from the depths of a rampant, masculine desire. 'I've never known a woman I couldn't keep my hands off—and, God, I've tried!'

He'd tried? When? she wondered hazily. Before they were married? Since?

His hand slipping under her sweater made her cry out. Those leather gloves were icy through the warm silk of her camisole. But the shock was short-lived as ice turned to fire, pain escalated into pleasure. Some primitive, abandoned impulse was wanting him to feed every sense, show her every sensation she could know with him, and in turn learn every secret delight of pleasing him.

'For goodness' sake . . . how long's it been?'

Days, she thought, glorying in the raw note of need in him that told her he was as frustrated as she was through having to curb their usual abandoned hunger for each other while Dawn had been staying with them. But now they would have the place to themselves, she realised, feeling that pulsing excitement as a sharp and painful throb way down inside, knowing that she'd be ready for him, that he would take her first without the need for any consideration before loving her again, with the slow and torturing ecstasy of his experience, as he whispered, 'Let's go back to the cottage.'

CHAPTER EIGHT

NADINE was in the middle of rearranging the sitting-room furniture in the London house when the telephone rang.

'Hi, it's me—Rachael. We met at the wedding. I haven't dragged you away from anything important, have I?'

Kneeling on the carpet, phone receiver in one hand, base in the other, Nadine had to stem a ridiculous urge to be on the defensive. 'No,' she answered politely, 'I was just moving some furniture. Rearranging things a little.'

'Getting nesting instincts?' Rachael's tone was decidedly patronising. 'Isn't it a recognised symptom of the last three months?'

'Is it?' Nadine queried, more abruptly this time. She didn't know what it was about Rachael Hampshire that always made her prickle with annoyance.

'You're not lifting anything heavy, are you?' Why did she sound so condescending, even when she was apparently showing concern? 'You wouldn't want to incur Cam's temper, now, would you? Because I think he'd blow his stack if he thought you were.'

'No, I do have some sense, Rachael,' Nadine couldn't help responding cynically, and, determined not to let herself stoop to the same tactics as her caller, asked in a cool, dismissive tone, 'Did you want to speak to Cameron? If so, I'm afraid he's back at his office today.'

'Of course. How silly of me. I was under the impression he was still on leave—that's why I've been trying the cottage. Your phone's out of order down there, did you know?'

'Yes, but it's working again now.' At least it had been before they had made a rather slushy journey back through the thawing snow yesterday, Nadine remembered, wondering why Rachael wanted to speak to Cameron.

'I only wanted to check that Cam got back all right the other day, because conditions were horrendous. At least, they were when he left me at that unearthly hour. Perhaps it wasn't so bad down there in Somerset.'

Nadine wasn't even aware of how tightly she was gripping the receiver. 'Yes. Yes, he got back all right,' she uttered, trying not to let the other girl realise that her statement had made its mark.

'Oh, good. Just as long as he's safe. That's all I was concerned about. Take it easy now, Nadine.'

She had rung off before Nadine even had time to respond, the conversation leaving her immobilised, cradling the receiver hard against her shoulder.

Had Cameron been with Rachael the other night? But why? she wondered, baffled. And why hadn't he said anything to her? Was that the reason he'd told her not to wait up—because he'd been planning on seeing the other woman? Had he really checked into a hotel or had that been an excuse because he'd spent the night with Lisa's lovely cousin?

Suspicion tortured her with cruel and crushing tenacity. Dear God! What was she letting herself believe? He was barely over Lisa, was he? Even if his moral and ethical codes had dictated that he should go through a marriage ceremony with *her*. And even if he *was* driven by an overwhelming passion for her, Nadine, it was only a chemical thing, divorced from the emotions and the intellect. It had nothing to do with love. And yet nor would his latent grief allow him to seek an affair elsewhere—piercingly she forced herself to face the reality of that much—and if she suspected otherwise, then all she had to do was ring the hotel where he'd said he'd stayed....

But she wouldn't let herself entertain a thought like that. It wasn't only mistrustful, it was downright paranoia! The best thing to do would be to ask him personally about it instead.

Disinclined to broach the subject immediately he came home, she waited until they had finished dinner, stacking the dishwasher before joining him in the drawing-room where he was reading a newspaper.

'What does Lisa's cousin—this . . . Rachael—do for a living?' She pretended to ask casually, though there was a little clutch of tension in her stomach as she sat on the settee opposite.

'Rachael?' She caught the surprise in his voice, felt the burn of his gaze, though she was feigning an interest in the recipe page of the magazine she had opened. 'She's a travelling sales executive. Why?'

Staring at the raspberry pudding topped with a creamy lemon sauce, Nadine held her breath. 'She's very lovely,' she supplied, keeping her tone light.

'Yes . . .' There was a contemplative twist to his mouth as he glanced absently at the top edge of his newspaper. 'I think half the men in London would probably agree with you.'

'Would you?'

'What's all this about?' He looked at her askance, those shrewd eyes narrowing. 'Has she been ringing you, by any chance?'

'Yes, she has.'

Did she imagine that sudden tightening of his jaw? 'To say what?'

Nadine shrugged nonchalantly, turning a page. 'Only to see if you got home all right.'

The newspaper rustled loudly as he tossed it abruptly aside. 'And what did you tell her?'

'That you did, of course,' she said with a dismissive little gesture. 'What did you want me to tell her? That I didn't realise you'd been with her? Why didn't you tell me?' It was an emphatic little plea as she threw closed her magazine. And then, more heatedly, 'Or wasn't I supposed to know?'

He fixed her with a hard look, those compelling eyes threatening to draw from her all the agony that was ripping through her heart. And then calmly he said, 'I didn't think my seeing her was important enough to mention. I had business with her——'

'*All* night?'

She hadn't meant to accuse him like this, but suspicion was eating away at her, and it was in no way appeased by the way his face suddenly hardened before he said, 'Is that what she told you?'

No, she hadn't. Not in so many words. But she couldn't refrain from uttering, through a poignant anguish, 'Well, she wouldn't have, would she? Oh, don't mind me! You can do anything you like. I didn't ask for any claim upon you, or for this marriage—you did! Only give me some idea of your private liaisons first, so that I don't look such an utter fool the next time one of your fancy women rings!' she snapped, tossing her magazine aside and jumping up.

'Come here!' She was all for ignoring the fierce impact of his command, but as she brushed angrily past him he rasped savagely, 'I said, come here!' catching her by the wrist and employing his knee to effect her soft, if undignified landing across his lap.

'Is that what you think Rachael is—my "fancy woman", as you call it?' He swore quietly and effectively. 'I've only recently lost one wife, for goodness' sake! And almost immediately—and much to her reluctance,' he slipped in with a grimace, 'taken another! Do you think I'm stupid enough to be looking for any other sort of involvement?'

She didn't know what he was looking for. Nor was she sure how he could have brought her so effortlessly into his arms. She only knew that his consuming warmth and his hard, arousing virility were calling to that insatiable need at the core of her being, inducing a panic in her that had her struggling against him for all she was worth.

'That careful little declaration doesn't change anything,' she uttered in a voice weakened by a tumult of
dangerous sensations, while her nails, sinking through
the fine silk of his shirt-sleeve, made no impression in
their need to hurt him—hurt him physically, as those
abject victims of his ruthless intellect in court must
sometimes surely have wanted to do in their frustrated
desire to move him, penetrate the impregnable.

'Oh, but it changes everything,' he whispered and,
swooping to claim her mouth, pressed her back until her
head touched the cushioned chair-arm, restraining her
by pinning her arms at the elbows, his mouth swallowing her protests until she lay panting and subdued
beneath him.

'Why would I want Rachael?' he asked quietly.

She closed her eyes, blotting out the seriousness of
his. It was what she'd asked herself from the moment
she'd found out, wasn't it? she berated herself. Because
the heated musk of his body, his warmth, his voice, were
like aphrodisiacs in themselves as his hands shaped the
flowering fullness of her body.

She was his wife, and though he might not love her
he wanted her—*her*! she stressed silently, fervently,
through her breath-quickening anticipation of arousal,
because his lips were working their dangerous magic on
her skin; that skilled hand was unfastening her blouse,
caressing the blossoming roundness of her breasts.

Dear heaven! If this was all she could have of him,
then let it be enough! And with a strangled murmur she
moved convulsively against him, knowing she was inciting his passion, despising herself yet glorying in her
own defeat, unable to do anything but follow where he
led, like a slave abandoning herself to the hedonistic
pleasures of her master.

The succeeding weeks passed with further falls of snow,
but nothing that settled, and a cold January rolled into
an even colder February that was only warmed by the
news one morning that the book Nadine had finished

typing for Cameron back in the autumn had been accepted for publication.

'Now your head's really going to swell,' she said, rolling her eyes as he finished reading the letter to her over the breakfast table. But she was secretly delighted, and proud of the very successful husband she had so recently married, and she allowed her joy at least to show, murmuring with a tantalising little smile, 'Are you going to take me out to celebrate this evening?'

The strong lines of his face were warmed by the satisfaction of success. 'I suppose, as you put so much work into it, you're entitled to some reward,' he teased.

'You make me sound like a chimp that's earned a grape!' she chided laughingly, the hands behind her head idly lifting her hair, unintentionally drawing that masculine regard to where her white robe gaped invitingly above her breasts.

'A she-cat. A tigress. A playful kitten. But never anything as unflattering as a chimp,' he stated, softening his disapproval with a smile. 'I must go, but, yes, we'll celebrate tonight.' He was on his feet, picking up the rest of his unopened mail, and some of the warmth went out of his smile as he studied one envelope before stuffing it, without opening it, into his trouser pocket.

'It's addressed to Lisa,' was all he said concisely, in response to her silent query, and she guessed that there would always be reminders—here in this same house where she'd lived. He had made no suggestion that they move, though, and she could only draw her own conclusions as to why he hadn't. Quickly she looked away, afraid of seeing something in his face that she didn't want to recognise—that dark edge of some deep personal emotion she'd noticed too often in his eyes and which was all the more intense for being so deeply concealed.

She rang him later that day to confirm the arrangements for the evening, but his clerk told her very politely that he wasn't in, although he'd left a number where he could be reached.

Reluctant to ring him on a personal matter while he was probably involved with a client, she left it until much later and then, having rung his chambers again without success, dialled the number the clerk had given her earlier.

The distinctive female voice that answered was unmistakable. Rachael Hampshire's!

Quickly and unthinkingly Nadine cut the line, instantly chiding herself for being so stupidly overdramatic. So what if he was at Rachael's? That didn't mean he was having an affair with the woman, did it? He'd hardly have left her number with his clerk if he was going to indulge in some torrid, clandestine passion, would he? She stilled her racing thoughts enough to realise this, and, pulling herself together, dialled Rachael's number again.

'Nadine! Was that you who rang off as soon as I answered just now?' She wasn't sure what Rachael was taking, but she sounded exuberant, as well as relishing letting Nadine know that she had guessed exactly why she had put the phone down as she had.

'Yes. I cut myself off,' Nadine fibbed, determined to save face. 'Is my husband there, by any chance? I'd like a quick word.'

'Your husband?' She made the word sound little more than a triviality. 'How formal!' Her little titter filled Nadine with the sudden shaming urge to strangle Rachael with her own lovely black hair. And then she said, with her voice coming more distantly, as though she'd turned away from the phone. 'Cam, darling. It's for you. It's your *wife*!'

Nadine heard his deep voice from somewhere in the background, and though she couldn't hear what he was saying she could gather, at least, that he didn't seem very pleased.

'Hello, Nadine.' His tone was cool and clipped. 'I'll be with you shortly. I was just leaving.'

With no explanation as to what he was doing there! she thought, fuming, unable to help saying waspishly, 'Are you sure you can tear yourself away?'

She heard the breath he drew in even over the line. 'I thought we'd been through this before. I'm not discussing it again. I told you. I'll be home right away.'

And that she had to be content with, she thought, and determined not to display any adverse feelings about it when he came home, regardless of how insecure it left her feeling inside.

The evening turned out to be pleasant in spite of that— an intimate meal with champagne in a first-class restaurant, over which Cameron displayed the charm and attentiveness that made him the perfect escort and companion, and during which she gave him the gift she had taken pains to choose for him that day.

'A gold pen?' A surprised smile touched his lips as he took it out of its little oblong box.

'I just thought it might improve your writing,' she said wryly, feeling the need for some justification in giving him such an expensive gift.

A dark eyebrow lifted in self-mocking agreement. 'Thank you,' was all he said softly, his hand covering hers across the table, his touch and the warm appreciation of his smile driving all thoughts of Rachael Hampshire from her mind so that silently she prayed, Dear God, please help me to make him love me!

But even in the throes of uncontrollable passion he had never told her that, had never even tried to pretend. And that night, as on so many others, she fell asleep in his arms, only to be troubled by disturbed and harrowing dreams.

She was a child again, standing at the gates to a deserted park, lost and alone, but she was a woman too, because she was pregnant, sitting in a crowded courtroom, with Cameron sitting beside her. Only he wasn't speaking to her. He was like a stranger, engaged in a silent battle in which she was the adversary, and Rachael Hampshire was sitting, smiling smugly, on his other side. Then, in the same second, she was the interrogated and he was the black-robed interrogator, pronouncing sentence and wrenching from her the infant she was cradling in her arms. She ran sobbing from the court. Only it didn't lead out into the street. It led into that deserted park, and she was that little girl again, standing heartbroken, frightened and alone.

'No!' She was suddenly fully awake, staring into the darkness, listening to Cameron's deep and regular breathing beside her. Her shocked gasp hadn't disturbed him and, having become disentangled from him in her sleep, she slipped quietly and easily out of bed.

A pale moon was washing the pastel walls of the little nursery adjoining their bedroom. The scent of a fragrant pot-pourri on the window-sill mingled with the smell of fresh emulsion. The added light from a street-lamp touched the far corner of the room and its yet-unoccupied cot, making a proud silhouette of the rocking-horse that stood near the window, which Cameron had recently had renovated, having had it brought up from the cottage.

The perfect stage, waiting for a new little character to make her entrance, she thought with a twisted little smile as she considered Cameron's desire for a boy. But what did it matter as long as it was healthy and happy...? The horse's mane was silky soft beneath her fingers. Happy? She dipped its head in gentle motion. It made an oddly comforting squeak. And it would be happy, wouldn't it? Heaven grant that it would never have to live under the threat of insecurity, of its world being torn apart, of those frighteningly vivid dreams...

'What are you doing out of bed?'

Startled, she glanced round, unaware of the very maternal figure she presented, standing there with one hand on the horse, the other pressed against her bulbous middle beneath the white towelling robe.

'The baby was kicking.' It was an excuse she could always use when she couldn't sleep, and anyway it was better than saying, I dreamt that you were taking it away from me. 'I'm sorry I woke you. I thought I'd managed to get out of bed quietly enough.'

'You did.' He spoke softly coming in, as though the night were sacred, hands thrust into the pockets of the dark robe he had thrown on which exposed his bare chest and legs. 'It was your mere lack of presence that disturbed me.'

She gave a little chuckle at that. 'In a minute you'll be saying I'm essential to you,' she said somewhat sceptically, unsettled by his comment. 'Or to your sleeping pattern, anyway.'

He gave a grunt of acceptance, dark head bowed towards her. 'Oh, but you are,' he said silkily.

His arm coming to rest on the horse's head as he came parallel with her made her realise how much taller he was than she, his response to the tentative little feeler she had put out a moment ago assuring her only of what she already knew. He was as enslaved physically by her as she was by him—except that his emotions didn't keep him awake as hers did. It was only the threat to that physical bonding that had the power to disturb him, nothing more.

'You know, when I was a child I was crazy about horses.' With a wistful smile she let her hand run over the small leather saddle. 'I used to put a cushion on the wall between us and the house next door, and sit astride it with a piece of string tied to our lilac tree for makeshift reins. I used to think that if I had a rocking-horse I could ride and ride it to some distant fantasy land, some safe, secure place where nothing and no one could ever reach me.'

'But you never got your rocking-horse.' His face, turned from the window, was in shadow and unreadable, but his tone communicated a deeper meaning than the simple statement conveyed. Did he understand, then, something of the turmoil she was going through? Because she knew in that moment the reason she had never wanted to marry, why she'd shunned relationships. Because she hadn't wanted to subject any child to the fear and insecurity she had suffered; because she had made an unconscious promise to herself that she never would. And now, through circumstances not altogether of her own making, she found herself not only pregnant, but trapped in a marriage without love.

'Come along,' he murmured quietly. 'Let's go back to bed.'

His hands on her shoulders turned her gently back towards the bedroom, and when they were lying down he held her against him without passion or any sign of desire, so that she fell asleep almost at once in the warm curve of his arm, clinging to a temporary illusion of immeasurable security.

The first signs of spring arrived towards the middle of the month, marked by a couple of milder days and the bright clumps of gold, white and purple crocuses dotting the London parks.

Nadine felt as though she had suddenly become huge, and, grimacing at herself in the mirror one morning, decided she looked it. She was only looking forward now, with excitement and a little apprehension too, to the day when the baby was born.

'It's a perfectly natural thing, having a baby,' Dawn Kendall had declared dismissively when Nadine had expressed some nervousness during one of her mother's visits. Dawn was more active now than she had been for a long time, and Nadine knew it was only the surgery that had enabled her to have that new lease of life. 'What about Cameron—is he going to be there when it's time?'

'I don't know,' Nadine had said quietly. 'He hasn't said.' And the truth was that she was too embarrassed to ask him, because in spite of sharing his house and his bed, sometimes he seemed very much like the cold, aloof stranger of her dreams.

'Maybe he doesn't want to, and I wouldn't blame him. I can't understand why there's such a modern trend for fathers being present at the birth. He did his bit months ago, and I think it's best for a man to see his wife and baby all clean and dignified,' Dawn had revealed, though it had come as little surprise to Nadine. It just tied in with her mother's rather antiquated ideas of men's and women's roles in marriage.

Yet even the most modern of wives would have found it irksome answering the phone during the times they were in together, only to have the caller ring off as soon as she picked up the receiver.

Rachael! she guessed intuitively, challenging Cameron about it when it happened one evening just as they were getting ready to go out.

'I wish you'd ask your girlfriend to stop ringing you here if she doesn't want me to know she's calling,' she couldn't help saying brittly as she resumed putting on her mascara at the dressing-table.

To her surprise, he laughed as he came out of the bathroom. 'All right. I'll tell her if she wants to ring me then she must do so at the office.'

Piqued that he couldn't see how it was upsetting her, Nadine swung round on her stool. 'I don't think that's particularly funny!'

'Oh, for heaven's sake, Nadine! She's Lisa's cousin. Like it or not, at the moment I'm afraid circumstances dictate that I have to have some contact with her,' he said casually, stretching his neck to adjust his collar above the perfect knot of his tie.

'I don't like her.' She hated having to admit it as she turned back to the mirror.

'I'm not asking you to.'

'So why does she keep ringing you?' Her mascara brush suspended, through the glass she saw him slip into his jacket before opening a drawer of the tall chest. 'Are you having an affair with her?' she demanded tremulously, laying aside her brush and swivelling round again.

'Do you really believe that?' He had his back to her and was studying the dark silk handkerchief he had just taken out of the drawer—Lisa's gift to him for his last birthday, she remembered—staring at it with a dark absorption before stuffing it into the top pocket of his jacket. 'Why the sudden preoccupation with my relationship with Rachael?' he enquired. Then, with a hint of mockery on his lips, 'Have you suddenly deluded yourself into thinking you're in love with me?'

Oh, God! That he should ever know that! she thought torturedly, lifting her head in defiance to hide that very vulnerable part of herself that knew she would die for him if he asked her to.

After a long pause he said quietly, his face like sculpted stone, 'No, I didn't think so—any more than you'd be prepared to believe I was in love with you.'

No, that was evident from the cold indifference in his face, Nadine realised, and with heart-wrenching pain watched him stride away from her, only to have her emotions stretched even more brutally when Rachael called round unexpectedly the following morning.

'Cameron isn't here,' she found herself saying without any preamble, as soon as she opened the door to Lisa's cousin.

'I know,' she said, and then, surprisingly, 'It's you I called to see. I happened to be driving past the end of the street so...' A little hand-gesture finished the sentence with a waft of subtly expensive perfume.

'In that case you'd better come in, though I can't pretend that this isn't an unexpected surprise...' Nadine didn't need to continue. She had known right from their first meeting—perhaps even before that, at Lisa's funeral—that Rachael considered herself a contender for Cameron's affections.

'Why should it be?' The girl was looking at her with almost doe-eyed innocence as she stepped inside. 'After all, we're sort of a family—in a way.'

'Are we?' Leading the way into the drawing-room, where she had been crocheting a hat for the baby, Nadine wasn't allowing herself to be taken in by Rachael's genial remark. 'I was under the impression the ties were all on Lisa's side.'

'Yes, well...' She shrugged, sitting down at Nadine's silent invitation, glancing towards the little green woollen garment on the opposite settee. 'You're making a bonnet. How lovely!' She couldn't have made it sound more useless, Nadine thought, if she'd been wallpapering a dustbin! 'You aren't expecting Cameron back soon, are you?'

'No, Rachael, I'm not.' Nadine eased herself down onto the sofa, feeling elephantine opposite Rachael, whose figure-hugging black suit and cerise satiny blouse had probably been selected from her wardrobe with that very purpose in mind, she considered waspishly. And before she had realised it she was saying in a surprisingly controlled voice, 'Why can't you leave him alone?'

Those beautiful doe-eyes instantly took on the she-hunter's calculating watchfulness. 'Has he said he wants me to?'

Of course he has! Nadine wanted to hurl at her. Only he hadn't. And this clever young woman knew it, she realised, her hesitation in answering only giving Rachael the greater confidence to say, 'He isn't happy, you know.'

For a moment, Rachael's staggering impudence left Nadine lost for words. Then, recovering herself, she managed to say with some degree of dignity, 'Oh, really? Has he told you that?'

Rachael nestled back into the cushions, completely at ease, self-assured. 'He doesn't have to. Anyone just has to look at him to see he's just acting out a role.'

Nadine stood up as quickly as she was able to, feeling clumsy and awkward. 'I think you'd better leave.'

'Why?' Unperturbed, Rachael crossed one long leg over the other, an open statement of her determination to stay. 'Because you know it's true? Oh, I know he had a nice, cosy little indiscretion with you—which is a bit milder than Lisa put it. And I must admit it did rather surprise me, knowing how crazy he was about *her*.'

An anguish pierced Nadine that she would rather have died than let Rachael see. That last remark had hurt more even than the knowledge that her old friend could have been so callous as to turn Nadine's intentions to help her into something so sordid and immoral. She was glad,

though, that Lisa's cousin didn't know the truth about
her baby's origins. The fact that they remained known
only to herself and Cameron helped her to respond
calmly, 'Just what are you getting at, Rachael?'

The other girl's smile was phlegmatic. 'Simply that
I'm fascinated to know exactly how you managed to
hook him. What did you do? Threaten him with a
massive paternity suit? Or did he simply feel it was his
duty to marry you?'

'That's quite enough!' Though she knew that last fact
was true, she couldn't let Rachael go on saying these
things, and tightly she uttered, 'I'm not going to stand
here and listen to any more of this! Quite honestly,
Rachael, all you're saying reeks of nothing but your own
unfortunate jealousy.'

'Jealousy?' She gave a brittle laugh. 'Hardly that. I
just happen to care about him, that's all. He was mine
before he was ever Lisa's. Oh, I see you didn't know
that.' It was a smug acknowledgement of Nadine's silent
surprise. 'I introduced them, fool that I was! I didn't
realise she wanted all the prestige of being his wife *and*
to play around as well. Poor Cam. He had to take the
double blow of discovering that and…well, you know…'
Casually Rachael threw out a hand, in subtle reference
to the accident. 'But it was me he came to for conso-
lation the instant he came back from France. Me he still
comes to. I suppose because he feels I'm a link with what
he's lost—which is probably why he's got you living here
in this house, if you think about it.'

Nadine didn't want to. Too often she'd wished they
could have begun their married life somewhere that didn't
constantly remind her of just why Cameron had married
her, even though he had had the master bedroom completely refurbished during their honeymoon.

'He would have come back to me when he'd got over
her death,' Rachael was continuing, before Nadine could
tell her exactly what she thought of her opinions, 'if you
hadn't been so careless as to let him make you pregnant.
And, knowing Cam, he would have to do the proper

thing and make his baby legitimate, but I just thought you ought to know that I intend to see that he doesn't sacrifice his entire life to you.'

Hands planted firmly on her hips, Nadine had to steel herself not to say something totally unladylike and unforgivable. 'You make it sound as though I dragged him chained and protesting to the registrar,' she responded drily, refusing to rise to Rachael's cruel baiting. After all, it had been virtually the other way around!

'Only because I know how deeply he felt about my cousin, despite his meaningless little escapade with you. And because I know that when Lisa was taunting him once, about secretly wishing he could run away with you, he told her that you'd served your purpose—whatever that was supposed to mean. Getting a hot-blooded fling out of his system, I suppose. And he said that marrying you was the last thing he wanted. Lisa might have been as mixed up as a triple cocktail, but one thing my cousin never did was lie to me.'

Only she had about Cameron having an affair with her, Nadine thought with an unbearable ache in her chest, taking little solace from the fact that Lisa would probably not have wanted anyone—even her cousin—to know that she'd arranged for someone else to provide a baby for her and Cameron while all the time she was carrying on with another man.

'Maybe your cousin didn't tell lies, but you certainly seem to have a remarkable talent for it, Rachael,' she uttered with a tight little laugh. She was unable to imagine Cameron saying such a thing, but doubt was a gnawing parasite way, way down inside.

'Do I? All right, if you don't believe me, ask Cam himself. Go on—ask him. He probably wouldn't deny it. You know the code of the great Cameron Hunter— the truth, the whole truth, and nothing but the truth. Go on, I dare you,' she invited silkily, getting up. 'If you're that sure of him you've got nothing to lose, have you?'

But she wasn't sure of him, that was the problem, Nadine realised despairingly.

The things Rachael had said were still bothering her as Cameron drove them back from a colleague's house late that evening. The only thing she knew with any certainty was that he wasn't in love with her, even though he had insisted on their marriage...

'You're quiet.' His remark penetrated her thoughts as they were coming to the end of their journey. 'In fact, you didn't say a great deal all evening. Is anything worrying you?'

'No.' Biting her lip, Nadine stared out of the nearside window. Why couldn't she tell him the truth? Was it because she was afraid he might clarify the things Rachael had told her? Or simply that she was so convinced he couldn't have said them that it seemed pointless even bringing them up? 'I'm sorry,' she apologised in a small, clipped voice, uncertainty making her edgy. 'I didn't realise I was letting you down.'

'Did I say you were?' The glance he directed across the dark space that separated them was mildly puzzled. 'I thought you bore up exceptionally well with the rest of us talking shop all night.'

Their host had been a judge, whose wife was a magistrate.

'Especially through Cavenham's shrewd probing about the contents of my book. I must say I admire your capacity for subtlety—keeping the old devil wondering until he sees the thing in print. I see I'd be up against stringent competition if ever you found your way into court.'

In spite of everything, Nadine smiled at his drily delivered compliment.

'I also admire your loyalty.' Carefully he brought the Mercedes along the row of garages at the rear of the Georgian terrace. 'You didn't have to tell him you agreed with every point I made in that book.'

'Why not?' she argued, wishing she wasn't so affected by the sincerity of his approval. 'I did. And so will everyone else—layman or professional—with a gram of sense and an appreciation of justice.'

'Commendation, indeed.' That sensual quality to his voice should have warned her as he pulled up outside their own garage, and she shot him a wary look as he cut the engine, suddenly switched off the lights.

'Aren't you putting it away?'

His soft laugh made her nerves quiver with both fear and excitement. 'Of course. But first such laudatory praise at least deserves some reward.'

His mouth over hers was forcing her back against the head-rest, the hands pinning her to the seat finding too easily the front fastening of her dress and the heavy fullness of her breasts beneath their fine covering of lace.

'No, don't . . .'

He ignored her tense little protest, bending to press his lips against the creamy swell of one breast, murmuring with incidental casualness, 'And why not?'

Why not? Nadine breathed deeply, lashes pressed against the wells of her eyes as she savoured the exquisite pleasure of that warm mouth on her flesh, feeling herself sinking beneath the tide of yearning that rose from the heart of her femininity, made her groan in acquiescence as she opened her eyes to the dark velvet of his head against her breast.

Why not? A surge of self-disgust pulsed through her as she remembered what Rachael had said about her serving her purpose. Well, she was serving her purpose now, wasn't she? she thought grievously. Allowing him to use her as he liked? Knowing she had no will to resist his dynamic physical power over her? Allowing it because she loved him, while he felt not a scrap of love for her; the only purpose behind his skilful and devastating subjugation of her was his own guaranteed satisfaction in bed!

'No!' Roughly she pushed him away, clasping her dress together with shaking fingers. 'Why must you always get your own way? I said I don't want to and I meant it! I'm tired. I'm going to bed.'

She was out of the car before he had a chance to stop her, running through the small garden and fumbling with her door-key, imagining as she let herself in through the rear door that he would garage the car before joining her. She was surprised, therefore, when he came striding in through the darkness after her, before she had even reached the stairs.

'Why the sudden cold shoulder?' Light flooded the hall from one angry movement of his hand. 'I wasn't aware you'd objected to my having my own way—as you so crudely put it—before.'

At the foot of the stairs Nadine squinted painfully, the sudden brightness hurting her eyes.

'I don't see what all the fuss is about,' she endeavoured to say nonchalantly. 'Just because I said no...' Turning to go upstairs, she gasped when he caught her arm, pulling her back to face him.

'But your saying no isn't all we're talking about, is it?'

The stern lines of his face brooked no resistance now, and Nadine shifted uneasily.

'All right, if you must know I had a visit from your ever-persistent girlfriend this morning, and she and I had a most enlightening talk!'

'You must have!' he said grimly, though he didn't even bother contradicting her description of the other girl. 'And?'

Clenched fists planted on his hips, his very stance demanded her compliance, and, sticking out her chin to stave off his intimidation, she uttered, 'Have I been serving my purpose, sir, as satisfactorily as you'd intended?'

'What the hell do you mean?'

Face contorted with distaste, his hand came to rest on the deeply carved acorn at the foot of the balustrade, and for one moment hope flared in her that he didn't have a clue what she was talking about.

'Don't you remember? That's funny. Rachael seems to remember it very well!' Tell me it's a lie! her mind was crying, though she had to press on, challenging him to deny it. 'I'd "served my purpose", I believe you told Lisa. And what else was there? Oh, yes! Marrying me was the last thing you wanted.'

His grip tightened mercilessly around the carving, his mouth so grim she expected an admonishing tirade for even accusing him of such a thing. Then he took a breath and said with a quiet anger, 'Rachael had no right to discuss any conversation I might have had with Lisa with you.'

'Then it's true!' Nadine hadn't realised that she, too, was gripping the balustrade, but she clung to it now for support as she felt her legs threatening to give way.

'You may well look at me as though I'm something that crawled in up the wastepipe, but I had reasons for saying it——'

'Yes, I'm sure you did! God!' The small cry escaped her as she threw back her head. 'What a sacrifice it must have been for you, submitting to those rigid principles of yours and marrying me when you knew I didn't even want...'

Looking up at the ceiling, she shut her eyes tightly, clenching her teeth, trying to cope with the hurt, the humiliation. It had been bad enough when she'd simply known that he didn't love her. But that he thought so little of her as well...

'And why should anything I've said or done upset you so much if you have so little interest in being my wife, Nadine?' He moved up a stair, grasping her by the arms and saying roughly, 'Why the hell do you think I married you?'

'Because you had to!' Tortured she threw the words at him. And then, with a bitterness that hid her painful anguish, all the poignancy of her deepest fears, 'Because you knew it would make it easier for you to get custody of the baby once you'd forced me into it!'

For a few moments after that bitter accusation they just stared at each other. Nadine was flushed and tense, unable to define whether it was anger or pain behind the cold hostility she saw in Cameron. And eventually he said, 'You really despise me that much?'

Catching her breath, she wanted to cry out, I don't despise you. I love you! But pride insisted on the dignity she had nearly sacrificed in his arms, and when she didn't answer he said coolly, 'I think you'd better go to bed.'

Pride, too, demanded that she did so without a word. And though she lay there in the darkness aching, in spite of everything, for him to join her, he didn't, and in the morning she realised that she had cried herself to sleep, sensitive to the fact that whatever fragile warmth there had been between them had been destroyed.

CHAPTER NINE

WATCHING her mother sowing seeds in the small vegetable patch above the orchard, a little ray of warmth brightened Nadine's pale, sad features.

Whatever she had had to endure—Cameron's contempt, this forced marriage, even the pain of loving him—it had all been worth it, she reflected sighingly, to see her mother leading a practically normal life again.

She couldn't help wondering, though, as she turned back into the kitchen, what her own future would hold. It was obvious Cameron had realised that they couldn't live happily together, despite his strong views about children needing two parents and a stable home. That was all very well if the parents loved each other—only, they didn't. At least, not on one side, she mused, with a sudden dull ache beneath her ribcage.

He must have accepted that, which was why he'd raised no objection when she had suggested spending the last couple of weeks of her pregnancy there at the cottage. Although he drove down often, spending odd nights there during the week, their relationship remained tense and strained, so that he seemed more companionable and relaxed with her mother than he did with her. And though he shared her bed still, he showed no inclination to touch her, simply turning over and allowing sleep to claim him as soon as he switched off the lamp, usually leaving the following day even before she was awake.

'Something's not right between you two, is it?' Dawn had observed, only that morning after Cameron had left. 'What is it, darling? Is it anything you want to talk about?' And then worriedly, with maternal fingers touching her daughter's cheek, 'You aren't having any regrets?'

Nadine had had to struggle not to give in and tell Dawn Kendall all that was bothering her. But looking at her mother and noting the absence of that drawn, tired look, the comparative ease of her breathing, she had whispered, 'No, I've no regrets.'

How could she confess what was troubling her anyway? Tell her mother that her husband didn't love her? That he preferred the company of someone else who was a link with the woman he'd really loved?

'I need to do some shopping.' She essayed a bright smile, forcing herself to look ahead as Dawn came in now. 'Get a few things for when I go into hospital. I'm going in to Bath.'

'What! In your condition?' Dawn protested, aghast.

'Don't worry. I'll get a taxi—there and back,' Nadine promised, already under strict orders from Cameron—though unnecessarily, she thought—not to drive herself around now that she was so near the end of her term. And she knew her mother would tell him if she did. Despairingly she had to accept that Dawn had become his greatest ally as she declined her mother's offer to go with her, not wanting to overtire her unnecessarily by dragging her round the shops.

What she hadn't reckoned on was feeling so tired herself after she had finished her shopping. Well, not really tired, she thought, after some consideration, just a bit weary. And she had an ache way down in her lower back which wasn't helping very much.

It was a lovely day, though, and as it was nearly lunchtime, she bought herself some sandwiches and took them down to eat them on a seat in the park. And that hadn't been such a good idea, she realised, gazing at a wondrous display of daffodils on a grassy mound in the centre, because being so alone—even though there were other people around—gave her too much time to think. And thinking hurt. Thoughts like, where did they go from there—her and Cameron? Was he waiting until the baby was born to tell her that he'd made a mistake? That it wasn't going to work?

How could she have known, when she'd stood on that bridge last summer, she thought, glancing towards the cavernous arches above the foaming river, that it wasn't possible, just because you loved someone, to expect them to love you back if they didn't want to?

'Nadine!' A familiar voice jolted her out of her painful reverie to see the tall man who had stopped and was smiling down at her. 'What a lovely surprise. May I join you?' The perfect gentleman, Simon Braith did just that as she smiled her assent. 'You looked down in the dumps,' he said gently. 'On such a lovely day, too. Getting a bit fed up with waiting?' His gaze embraced her ample middle beneath the simple green maternity dress she wore under her creamy jacket. 'How long is it now?'

Glad to see a friendly face, Nadine answered with a grimace, 'Two weeks—and counting every day!'

'I'll bet you are—and Cameron too,' he remarked sagaciously. 'How is he?'

'Fine.' Forcing herself to sound brighter, so that Simon wouldn't guess at the problems they were having, she added, 'He's having a busy time. He's been involved on a complicated case this week, and after court closes today he's flying straight off to Manchester to see a client tonight.' And she wouldn't see him because he was staying over in Manchester—a trip he was probably relieved to be making, she thought unhappily, probably seeing it as a respite from the disastrous farce of his marriage.

'He's overworking,' Simon was commenting surprisingly. 'Although I wish I had some of his energy, as well as his resilience. After the way Lisa treated him——' he spoke quietly, as though it wasn't quite politic to be mentioning her name '—I'm surprised he even feels inclined to bother sorting out this fiasco for her cousin.'

A line pleated Nadine's forehead. She couldn't tell him she didn't know what 'fiasco' he was talking about as she stared at the bright pink blossom of an early-flowering cherry tree across the river. But she knew, even if Simon didn't, why Cameron wasn't needing any persuasion to be with Rachael.

'She's very beautiful.'

'So I gather.' His mouth twitched at one corner and Nadine shivered beneath her light jacket, wondering whether Cameron had told him that. 'I believe Cameron's had his work cut out, though. Not only trying to sort out the legal side with this chap who's been trying to swindle her, but also having to restrain her heavyweight boyfriend from taking the law into his own hands and using actual physical violence on the rogue himself.'

'Her...' Pulling a strand of hair out of her eyes, Nadine tried to look anything but surprised.

'Very big and very possessive—so I'm led to understand.'

Then Cameron *wasn't* looking for comfort in her arms. Not with a heavyweight boyfriend lurking about, he wouldn't be! Now a little bubble of laughter escaped her. For the first time in weeks it sparkled in her eyes and a flush touched her cheeks, making her skin glow against the wild fire of her hair.

'Yes, he's had a lot to contend with recently,' Simon was saying, 'what with ... Lisa—and then the accident. A weaker man would probably have cracked under the strain. I'm glad he's been able to put the past behind him now, though, and can start to look forward to enjoying himself with his new little family. He's too tough on the outside to admit anything—even to me—but back last year, sometimes I thought I'd never seen any man so lost in himself——'

He broke off quickly, as though he'd said too much, and a swift, sharp pain went through Nadine. She knew how much he'd loved Lisa. Hadn't Rachael told her? Hadn't she seen it for herself? Only, hearing Simon saying something like that just seemed to hammer it home.

'I'd better get back.' Quickly she shook the crumbs from the cellophane wrapping on to the grass for the birds and stood up, stuffing the wrapper diligently into her bag.

'Going straight home?' Simon was already on his feet. And when she nodded, he asked, 'Did you drive in?'

'No,' she laughed, guessing at his intention to escort her to wherever her car might be. 'Both Cameron and my mother have conspired to see that I don't! I came by taxi.'

'Quite rightly too.' He smiled. 'So the least I can do is get you a taxi home.'

'No, that's all right, really...' Graciously she tried to wave aside his offer. She needed time alone. Time to think. But just like Cameron he was taking control.

Which was probably what made them such firm friends—that mutual strength of character, she thought as he flagged down a taxi just as they were approaching the bridge, and, with a 'Regards to Cameron', supplied the driver with the cottage address and bundled her inside.

So Rachael had a boyfriend, and one which Cameron knew about, she reflected, still reeling from the shock as the car whined into motion. She'd as good as accused him of having an affair with her, entertaining suspicions and doubts which had only been exacerbated by Rachael herself, it was true. And why Rachael had said those things she didn't know—except that the girl must have been eaten up with jealousy. A jealousy that had only been fuelled by the knowledge of how much he had loved her cousin, and therefore he could hardly be in love with her, Nadine.

But if Lisa's ghost was all she had to fight, then she could cope with that, now that she knew that Rachael Hampshire wasn't in the running. And perhaps if she hadn't been so ready to accuse him of imprudent liaisons with the other girl—made that awful accusation about him marrying her solely for custody; if she'd swallowed her pride and shown just one glimmer of affection, perhaps one day he might have...

As the taxi purred smoothly through the busy streets she quickly stemmed the wild tide of her thoughts. Hadn't he also as good as admitted that he'd said marrying her was the last thing he'd wanted? Well, of course it would have been, when he'd had Lisa, she thought, with a searing emotion adding to the continuing discomfort in her lower back.

She only knew she was aching for her husband to come back, desperate to see him again, to kiss goodbye to her foolish pride and apologise for all those dreadful accusations she'd made, knowing that that would be a start. Only he wasn't coming home. He was flying off tonight, after which time he might decide that he preferred it away from her after all, and she could lose him for good.

Gripped by an inner panic, she was delving into her handbag. She had very little cash left. But she did have her cheque-book and credit cards, and at least enough money for a reasonable tip...

'I want to change my mind.' Urgently she was leaning forward to the driver. 'Could you take me to the law courts?'

'Trim Street?' With abrupt efficiency he was already changing lanes.

'No,' she said, and with chin-lifting determination, 'I mean the law courts, London. Off the Strand.'

'You're joking?' Through his rear-view mirror, the man was looking at her as though he had a madwoman on his hands, and when she didn't answer, unsure herself whether she was doing the right thing, he said dubiously, 'Do you know how much it's going to cost you?'

Only her pride, she thought. But what was that against the possibility of saving her marriage?

After her assurance that she could pay his fare, and, when he had expressed further tentative worries, that she wasn't likely to give birth in the back of his taxi, he finally agreed to take her.

They stopped only at the motorway services so that she could ring her mother—who took quite a lot of placating when Nadine told her what she was doing—but it was still well into the afternoon when they eventually pulled up outside the courts.

'Thanks.' Hurriedly she scribbled the man a cheque, and, after giving him a generous tip and gathering her bags together, found herself thinking, as she came through the black gates, up the two flights of steps to the heavy double doors, of the last time she had done that—the day she had gone there to tell Cameron she was keeping the baby.

How nervous she had been then! And how little had changed! she thought wryly as her racing heart, combining with the baby in making her breathless, made her realise that even now her body still overreacted at the prospect of seeing him.

Within seconds she was checking the court list to see where Cameron would be, and, afraid of missing him if she waited in the hall, climbing the steep wooden steps to the upper floor.

Sculpted arches spanned the corridor, flanked on one side by the leaded windows and dark panelling of an awesome succession of courts, and catching the muted voices coming from the room where Cameron was defending, Nadine sank gratefully down on one of the ancient recessed benches beneath the arched window opposite, waiting for the afternoon session to finish.

After a while, though, she began to feel restless and fidgety. Her backache was getting worse, and, deciding she would be more comfortable inside the courtroom than out, very quietly she opened the door and crept up to the public gallery.

'What I'm *trying* to establish, m'lud, is whether or not the defendant was given the slightest opportunity...'

Even in the execution of its duty, Cameron's voice still sent a little frisson down her spine, along with a sudden gripping spasm of pain in her lower back that momentarily took her breath away and had her reproaching herself for her adventurous climb up those stairs. Perhaps she should have asked one of the security men if she could have used the lift!

'But that's just the *point* I'm trying to make!'

Listening to her husband's voice dominating the well-attended courtroom—silent save for the odd cough or the restless shuffle of feet—Nadine was glad that he hadn't noticed her, even though she was attracting attention from one or two members of the gallery with her voluminous size.

Her interest, though, lay only with the man who was commanding the full attention of the court. She was as transfixed as anyone by the pride and arrogance of that dark wigged head, by the sway of his robe as he swung back in cross-examination, by the ruthless calculation behind his hard enquiry as he demanded of a trembling witness, 'Did you or did you not deliberately seek out the defendant so that you could perpetrate——'

Suddenly he looked up and saw her. Their eyes locked, and for a second his registered—what? Nadine wondered, her heart lurching, because it was only for a second. But then, as though he had never seen her before, he turned away, his face a frigid mask, the cold, remorseless voice that carried on its merciless interrogation ripping through Nadine as though he'd just driven a stake through her heart.

Dear God! Did she have no power to move him? Was there nothing left to hang on to? Nothing at all? Heaven knew, she hadn't expected waves and cheers from him when he saw her, but something—some glimmer of recognition, something other than that rigid, icy disdain. Then something caught her eye, a movement that drew her attention down towards the back of the court, and a cold consternation seeped through her.

Rachael was sitting there, one slender arm resting on what looked like a flight-bag on the bench beside her, and as she glanced up at Nadine there was a kind of haughty triumph in her expression, filling Nadine with a startling feeling of *déjà vu*. And then she remembered. Her dream!

Was this, then, what it had been? A premonition? Cameron a stranger, with Rachael sitting there in court?

A silent hysteria gripped her. Simon had been terribly wrong. However strong Cameron's grief, it was still Rachael he needed. Rachael who had obviously packed to take a trip. And Cameron wasn't planning on coming home tonight.

A spasm of pain tore through her, so intense that she thought her silent anguish had extended itself to every last part of her being. But the pain was wholly physical, and as her arms flew to grasp her middle she heard her own agonised, involuntary cry.

'The baby...!'

Racked by the spasm, she heard the man beside her asking urgently what he could do to help, the judge demanding over the microphone, 'Who is that woman?' But she was gripped by too much pain to be truly aware of anything except the swirl of black robes as Cameron swept across the court, mounting the steps to the gallery like some dark flying demon out of hell.

'I'm sorry,' she sobbed against the dark sleeve of the arm he placed around her, leaning heavily against him, one half of her rejecting, the other welcoming the security he offered. 'I'm sorry, Cameron. I didn't intend this...'

'It's all right.'

But it wasn't. The court was in an uproar. People were turning to look at what was happening, talking speculatively among themselves, and above it all a very irate judge was thundering for silence with his hammer, while Cameron was trying to identify her to him, pressing him urgently for an adjournment.

'For God's sake! Someone ring for an ambulance!' In spite of that urgent command he seemed remarkably in control as he turned to Nadine, asking in cool, clipped tones, 'What is it? Is it the baby?'

As the pains subsided a little she nodded. 'It's coming,' she breathed, her voice tinged with a mixture of fear and disbelief. Hadn't everything she'd read about first-time pregnancies suggested that babies often came later than expected? That there was always plenty of warning...?

'What are you doing here anyway?' Cameron wanted to know, looking worried as he got her into a private room to wait for the ambulance to arrive. 'Has something happened to your mother?'

She shook her head, saying only, 'It doesn't matter,' because she couldn't tell him now. Her suspicion that he had been planning to go away with Rachael had only been confirmed when the girl had come up to them with a superficial concern for Nadine as he had been helping her from the court.

She had been unable to avoid overhearing his quietly rasped, 'I'm afraid you're on your own now, Rachael. Call me when you get back.'

But she couldn't think about that now, because everything was happening so fast. In no time at all, it seemed, she was in the hospital, in more pain than she had ever known before. But the pain was emotional, too, because although Cameron had been with her in the ambulance, for some reason he wasn't there now, and she needed him. Oh, God! How she needed him now!

She closed her eyes, gritting her teeth against the pain, her nails sinking hard into the hand someone slipped into hers. But surprisingly that hand didn't flinch. Looking up, she realised it was Cameron, and that he'd been there all along. It was all she could do to stop herself crying out his name. And then, just when she thought she couldn't take any more, it was all over, the pain and the agony forgotten in the unsurmountable joy of hearing her baby's cry.

* * *

She was resting against the pillows, looking much more presentable, when Cameron came back from telephoning her mother—which would have met more with Dawn's approval, she thought with a grimace, wondering what her mother would think about Cameron having been present in the delivery-room.

He was still wearing the dark suit he had been wearing in court, only his tie was pulled loose, the collar of his shirt unbuttoned. There was a day's shading around that jutting jaw, and he looked dark around the eyes, too. As though he'd been pushing himself too hard, Nadine thought, remembering something Simon had said about him overworking in what seemed another lifetime. And in spite of everything her heart twisted with the strength of her love for him as he sat down on the bed, so that she uttered quietly, 'Thank you for being there.'

She didn't realise how much of a favour she had made it sound until a black eyebrow arched incredulously.

'It's my child, for heaven's sake!'

'It's also a girl.' Nadine gave a little shrug beneath the plain white cotton nightie the hospital had supplied her with. And added with a little hint of bitterness, 'Does that mean you're going to send her back?'

A shadow seemed to flit across his face as painfully she reminded him of his teasing remarks during that walk in the snow back in the winter, and with a glance towards the little crib he said wryly, 'Did she come with a receipt?'

'No, I didn't have time to ask for one,' she responded with a little less poignancy.

'In that case we're going to have to keep her, aren't we?' he said drily.

His gaze was so direct that she couldn't meet it levelly, feeling strangely embarrassed, and hurting too, because he'd said 'we' again, just as he'd done in the delivery-room, when he'd praised her so effusively on her efforts and told her that they'd got a little girl. But surely he couldn't have meant it, she thought, in the way she wanted him to? Glancing up at the clock above the door of the private little ward, she said tentatively, 'Shouldn't you be in Manchester?'

'No.'

But you would have been, she thought grievously, if the baby hadn't stopped you. In Manchester—with Rachael.

'Isn't it reasonable to want to spend some time with my daughter?' he said softly. Then, with a smile, 'We can hardly call her Patience, can we?' In fact the midwife had confirmed that she'd come remarkably quickly for a first.

'I'm calling her Justine.' With a movement of red waves she stuck out her chin determinedly, half expecting him to object, but his mouth merely firmed in consideration of her choice.

'As the nearest thing to justice?' he enquired with a twinge of irony. 'Because she's the only thing you got out of this marriage that you really wanted? Or because she first made her presence felt in court and you're hoping she'll follow her father to the bar?'

'No.' The flicker of amusement she saw in his eyes made her lift her chin higher. 'Because I want her to be everything that's fair and open-minded and honest,' she stressed, in a way that earned her an oblique glance from him.

'You say that with a touch of bitterness.' Reaching across, he tilted her averted gaze to his, his fingers light against her jaw. And the tell-tale glistening of her eyes prompted him to say softly, but firmly, 'I've never lied to you, Nadine. Only perhaps by omission, but to have told you the truth...' That ominous pause as he got up and moved away from the bed filled her with a chilling apprehension.

'Well...' He shrugged as he turned around, hands stuffed into his trouser pockets. 'Of course I told Lisa that marrying you was the last thing I wanted—I was already married, for heaven's sake! And I wanted to make my marriage work—not see it all go down the drain. But after that weekend I spent with you, heaven only knows how I stopped myself picking up the phone and ringing you. I wanted to. God! I wanted to! In fact, once I went as far as dialling your number and cutting it dead before you could answer. I thought I was going crazy—on the brink of throwing away everything I was trying to hold together for——'

He stopped short, taking a deep breath, and woundedly she supplied, 'Sexual attraction?'

For a long moment his eyes held hers, and she almost believed she could see pain as consuming as her own in their blue depths before he said, exhaling heavily, 'Yes.'

Well, what had she expected him to say? It was only the truth, she thought achingly. And it hurt. His admission, though, that he had wanted to do something about it—had nearly broken every rule and telephoned her at a time when she had been castigating herself over her own guilty desperation to hear from him—surprised her. The fact that he hadn't just showed the formidable strength of his character.

'Anyway, it wouldn't have been right then.' He had moved over to gaze out of the window at the night sky, the dark slope of his shoulders blocking out the line of illuminated windows on the building opposite.

'No,' she accepted resignedly, lying back against a mountain of pillows. 'It would have been foolish when you thought you had a happy marriage and...' And though it hurt excruciatingly to say it, she did, 'And a wife you loved.'

Those shoulders seemed to tense, rigid beneath his jacket, as though he had taken a breath and forgotten to let it out. Finally he turned round, and there was a gaunt, tight look to his features. 'I never loved Lisa,' he shocked her by saying categorically then. 'I know that now. I suppose—if I'm honest—I even knew it at the time.'

'But you...' Dumbfounded, Nadine gazed disbeliev-ingly up at him, not sure she had heard him correctly. 'But you married her,' she murmured, sitting up again.

His mouth twisted self-derisively. 'I thought we had a lot in common,' he said in a cold, flat tone. 'She was also witty, intelligent, vivacious. Even with all that, though, I still wouldn't have married her if she hadn't led me to believe she was pregnant. But she knew, be-cause of the way I felt about children, that I would stand by her. In marrying her I thought I could build the secure home I'd never had. I didn't realise I was being blindly and effectively tricked. Oh, she was tearful enough, and made every available excuse as to why she had done it when I eventually found out, and I tried to make a sincere go of it, but then, when it was confirmed that she couldn't actually have a baby, she started going off the rails. Our marriage was already rocky by the time you agreed to...' He didn't have to spell it out.

'I knew she was attracted to other men, but I really believed there were maternal instincts in her some-where—that a child would ultimately stabilise our mar-riage—save Lisa from herself.' Those strong hands made an empty gesture that revealed the hopeless futility of it all.

'I'm sorry,' Nadine whispered, and she was. But she was facing the torturous memory of Rachael sitting there in court waiting for him, which meant that if he hadn't loved Lisa, as he'd just admitted, then Rachael must have been right when she'd said that if he hadn't made her, Nadine, pregnant, he would have wanted *her*.

'Cameron...we've got to talk...about the future.' It was like having spears driven into her to say it, and every ounce of her anguish was written on her face as she looked up at him with wide, tortured eyes. She won-dered if it was the thought of his beautiful Rachael waiting for him when he couldn't go to her that was responsible for that dark, suppressed emotion in his.

'Yes,' he said on a heavily rasped breath, as though he was finally accepting too that it took more than a child to hold two people together. 'But not now. You aren't in any condition to think about that now. Wait until you're home.'

CHAPTER TEN

HAVING finished the seemingly eternal task of feeding and getting Justine off to sleep again, Nadine was just trying to persuade Tuesday, who was curled up against her feet, to move so that she could take her little daughter upstairs when Cameron drawled unexpectedly from the lounge doorway, 'That cat should be out doing what all good cats do best—annoying some other poor defenceless creature!'

But he was smiling that lazy, indulgent smile and Nadine's heart leaped. He was usually in court—or in chambers—at this time of the morning and he looked vitally fresh and intensely masculine in a light, well-cut suit that strongly emphasised the dark olive of his skin.

'There aren't as many rabbits for her to chase here in London as there are around the cottage,' she said lightly, getting up, her gaze feasting on the dark velvet of his hair as he stooped to pet her now languorously stretching cat.

'Nevertheless, you'll have to instruct both your little dependants to realise that some of your time belongs to the master of the house,' he chided softly, straightening again.

She gave an awkward little laugh, and felt that old, familiar stirring in her blood. He hadn't sought much of her time over the past few weeks, and yet there had been no further calls from Rachael. And on those occasions when they had been alone—Dawn had been staying with them since the baby was born—Nadine realised that she, too, had deliberately tried to occupy herself with things that would take her away from him, as though, for both of them, avoiding each other could delay the inevitability of things that still remained unsaid.

'What are you doing home anyway?' A careful glance at her watch on the arm supporting little Justine showed that it was barely midday. 'You aren't usually around at this time of the day.'

'No. I decided it was time you had a couple of hours to yourself. Go and get ready. I'm taking you out to lunch.'

'But the baby...' Anxiously Nadine looked down at the sleeping infant as Cameron came with her across the hall. One tiny fist was curled against her chest and her eyes were tightly closed, the determined little face flushed beneath its crown of rich brown hair—a perfect blend of her own fiery red and the rich, dark gloss of Cameron's. 'Supposing she wakes up?'

'I think your mother's had some practice in looking after babies,' he commented drily. 'Besides, we need this time, Nadine.' And as she met the sobriety of his features, wondering at that sudden seriousness in him, he said quietly, 'It's important,' so that a small, tight knot made itself felt in the pit of her stomach.

Of course. She had known the time would have to come eventually; the moment she'd been dreading ever since that day in the hospital. It was just that she wasn't ready for it, that was all.

The sun shone warmly through the car windows on to the pale cream jersey suit she had changed into as Cameron brought them out into the countryside, but it was a changeable sky, with dark clouds laying dramatic emphasis on the bright splashes of spring colour.

Cups of red and yellow tulips stirred in gardens and on snatches of well-tended council land, the white and pink blossom crowning the trees as they passed through a village vying with the spectacularly dark red of a dominating copper beech. Primroses still dotted the hedgerows, and as they turned a corner a forsythia bush in the driveway of a house stood out against the dark sky like fluorescent gold.

The Mercedes was pulling off the road and Nadine's stomach clenched tightly, her gaze darting questioningly to Cameron as he drew up outside the small, country hotel.

'Why did you bring me here?' Tension laced her words. How could he? she wondered, staring up at the diamond-paned windows overlooking the quiet, rambling grounds. Here, where they had spent that first weekend together?

He shrugged, appearing totally unaffected, and that made it worse. 'It's as good a place to eat as any.' He sent her a swift, speculative glance as he took the keys out of the ignition. 'Do you mind?'

Nadine shook her head, her hair moving softly against the taut, pale structure of her face. How could she tell him it was stripping her heart raw just being there?

'No,' she murmured, striving for the impartiality that came so naturally to him. 'Why should I?'

He didn't say anything as he got out of the car, the hand at her elbow impinging as he guided her over the crunching gravel to the front entrance. But when they were inside, moving along the familiarly carpeted corridor to the small dining-room, he said matter-of-factly, as though he had guessed at the tension that was knotting her stomach muscles, 'The one sure way to get rid of ghosts, Nadine, is to lay them.'

'Is that what you're doing?' She spoke breezily as she sent a glance across her shoulder, even managing a smile. 'Laying ghosts?'

He didn't answer, and as he pushed open one of the swing-doors for her into the dining-room she caught the stabbing fragrance of his cologne.

A waiter leaped instantly forward to direct them to their table. It was near the panoramic window that offered a view of the garden, and was intimately laid for two, a small vase of carnations in the centre adding a touch of colour to the creamy cloth and silver cutlery.

'Thanks.' She was barely aware of the waiter pulling out her chair, or of the contents of the menu with which he supplied her, because of the stabbing knowledge of having sat at this table before. Only then she had had no appetite for a different reason—the unrelenting tension that had racked her because the darkly charismatic man across the table, who had unnerved and intimidated her with his implacable authority, his sophistication and that eternally dangerous allure for her, had been going to take her to bed.

Unwittingly she looked up, and saw the hard, cynical line of his mouth, as though he was remembering too, and, caught in the riveting intensity of his gaze, she said falteringly, 'You arranged this deliberately, didn't you?'

He made a half-contrite movement with his mouth. 'The hotel—yes. The table—no. If you want to I can arrange for us to move, though I fail to see why. Since there was no sentiment attached to our compelling physical obsession for each other, it shouldn't prove to be anything more than a minor irritation for you.'

Nadine felt her breath come like a drawn knife across her lungs. Was that how he had seen their lovemaking? As a compelling physical obsession?

Every part of her wanted to lash out at him for his insensitivity, scream out that it had meant more, much more to her than that. But, striving for the same detachment, she merely shook her head and uttered with a feigned carelessness, 'As you said, hardly enough to constitute a move.'

With a cool circumspection his eyes were assessing her across the table, and unable to bear it, feeling as if she would break beneath the stripping intensity of his regard, she said quickly, 'Did you bring me here to talk about anything in particular?' As if she didn't know! 'You said it was important...' The tightening knot in her stomach was making her feel almost sick.

'Let's at least eat first,' he rasped, his voice surprisingly clipped now.

But she couldn't. Even when the waiter took away her half-finished soup and brought the simple cheese and pineapple salad she had ordered she could only pick at the moist golden portions of fruit and the shredded vegetables with a lack of interest that unintentionally aroused Cameron's concern.

'Not hungry?' he commented with a tilted survey of the food she was toying with, of her proud, tightly disciplined features.

'No, not very.'

'Eat it,' he advised, his words strung with a command. 'I know you want to get your figure back, but that isn't the way to do it.'

What do you care? she thought achingly, glancing out at the garden. It was laid to grass, with a sundial in the centre, and the fresh wind was tossing the petals of some exposed tulips across the lawn.

'Cameron...'

'I know.'

Quickly Nadine raised questioning eyes to his. How did he know what she had been going to say?

'It's ludicrous to go on the way we've been going.'

'Yes.' She wondered how it was so easy to agree with him when her heart was breaking.

'I have to admit to being wrong. One parent is preferable to two who live together like strangers under the same roof.'

Nadine felt as though something was blocking her throat as she tried to swallow. 'What are you saying?' She already knew the answer to that.

He didn't respond for a moment, then quietly he said, 'You didn't have to marry me, you know.'

'*No*?' It was a bitter little laugh. If he hadn't forced her to then she wouldn't have become so deeply involved with him. A parting would have hurt, it was true, but she'd have survived. But now... 'You said if I didn't you were going to take Justine away from me. You said you wouldn't be able to stop the facts coming out about why she was conceived.'

Something flared in his eyes before they became storm-dark, all emotion obscured like a ship shrouded in mist. 'Yet you would have given her up,' he remarked with a calculated precision, 'if Lisa and I had——'

He didn't even need to finish. Her chest feeling as though it was locked in a vice, Nadine glanced unconsciously up at the ceiling beyond which Justine had first come into being, and, thinking of the daughter she was longing to get back to, she murmured with painful honesty, 'It would have killed me.'

'So now you want your freedom and an assurance that you can keep her?'

It was like a whiplash, the sting of which she almost physically recoiled from. Wasn't it *his* freedom he was talking about? The freedom to be with Rachael?

'You have to promise me that,' she said, her voice unavoidaby shaking, subdued by the nightmarish reality of what was happening to her marriage. She'd done everything to avoid this union in the beginning. And yet now that it was finished . . .

'I think we'd better go.' There was a strange rigidity to Cameron's voice, a sombre intensity to his features. Possibly, she thought, he had recognised the numbing misery that seemed to be engulfing her and was keen to avoid a scene in public. And of course he would have regrets—about making another mistake, seeing a second marriage founder, if nothing else.

By the time they were back in the car she had regained a degree of self-composure. She would need it, need all the mental strength she could hang on to until after he'd sorted out the arrangements for her and Justine, she thought as he started driving her back, and wondered with a harrowing anguish how soon he would want her to leave.

She was still lost in her troubled thoughts when he pulled up on the side of the road. They must have turned off the main road earlier, and she hadn't noticed it, because this one was hemmed on either side by trees and high hedges, she realised through a numbing inertia. She was only stirred by the soft command in Cameron's voice as he said, 'Come on. A walk will do you good.'

Dappled sunlight filtered through the trees on to the path as he casually took her arm, guiding her along past the high hedges beyond which the odd exclusively designed house peered privately out from its own immaculate grounds. At the end of the quiet cul-de-sac the hedges ended abruptly, giving on to a low-walled garden partially hidden by trees and rhododendron bushes, where a straggling wistaria, only just beginning to blossom, climbed a tall wrought-iron gate.

As Cameron stopped suddenly, Nadine looked distractedly through the ironwork. The spectacular cream of magnolia blossoms made a vivid contrast against the red brickwork of a house smaller and older than its neighbours, although it looked empty, the garden returning to nature, almost unkempt.

'You'll need somewhere to live,' she heard Cameron saying in a cool, detached voice, 'and this——' surprisingly, he was pushing open the gate, gesturing for her to go through '—is about the best I can provide for you and Justine. I thought you wouldn't want to live too far away from your mother, yet on the other hand I'm keen that our daughter doesn't grow up in the city itself.'

Stepping through into the quiet garden, Nadine looked at him with wounded surprise. They had talked about that before once, when she had laughingly told him that her dream house would be somewhere hidden out of view in the countryside with easy access to London. This place could easily have come up to fulfilling that dream, she thought, looking absently around the wild garden and wondering what sort of rent he was going to have to pay for a property like this. Except that now she could feel no joy in imagining herself living there.

'It's big,' was all she was able to utter without giving herself away.

He grimaced. 'Well, yes. I don't intend relinquishing my right of occupancy entirely.'

'You mean...' Her pulse was suddenly throbbing hard. 'You can't——'

'Can't I?' he stated grimly. 'A man needs visiting rights to his daughter—and far better that she sees me in her own home rather than be dragged away from her friends and familiar surroundings every weekend, like a lot of other split-parent kids.'

He couldn't be saying this! Suddenly anger flooded through Nadine. How could he contemplate such a thing—leaving her and then coming back, with absolutely no regard for her or her feelings, whenever he thought fit?

'And what would you do? Bring Rachael too?' she enquired astringently, praying that her voice didn't reveal how much she was hurting inside. 'Those would be fun weekends! And how, exactly, would you explain them to Justine?'

'I wouldn't need to,' he said decisively, and seeing her puzzled look he went on to clarify, 'I wouldn't be bringing Rachael. That obsession I spoke of, Nadine, is still very much alive and kicking, and if we've got nothing else, there'll never be a third party who's going to interfere with that.'

'You mean, you...' Flabbergasted and hurt that he could even dream of using her in such a way, and seeing the intent on his face as he started purposefully towards her, she backed away with a frightened, 'No!'

'Yes,' he said savagely, grabbing her as she stumbled back against the gate and the sparse blue petals of the wistaria bush, and she couldn't protest because his mouth was suddenly bearing down on hers.

Every instinct rebelled against proving him right, but his kiss was insistent, giving her breath only so he could hungrily savour the taste of her neck, her face, her hair.

His hands roughly moulded her slim body to the crushing strength of his, evoking that wild desire in her that left her breathless and panting, a slave to her devastating love for him, against her wishes, her reasoning, her will.

'Rachael—Lisa! No matter who you thought I loved you'd still melt for me, Nadine. Just like you did the first time—just like you're doing now! Your sexual chemistry's so bound up with mine you'd surrender to me no matter what I did. No matter what your brain was advising you against me you'd still want me, wouldn't you?' And tugging her head back by her hair, as though he would drag a response from her if he had to, he growled fiercely, 'Wouldn't you, Nadine?'

'Yes.' Eyes closed, driven by her need, she hated herself for her weakness, and yet there was no point in denying it when her body was responding to those rough hands with a will of its own, expressing its wanting in its own primeval and instinctive arching towards him as she sobbed another involuntary, 'Yes.'

'So why?' His face drawn into barbarous lines, he almost shook her, willing her to look at him. 'Why does it hurt you to think I'm with Rachael when you know that I'm no more capable of withholding what you want from me than you are of resisting it? That that part of me you want, you can have—that it's always been yours——'

'Cameron, don't...' She couldn't bear it! Violently she struggled for her freedom, and was surprised by how easily he let her go.

'Why not? Because you're too damn proud to admit you love me?'

Eyes stung by tears, she turned from the blurred blue carpet of forget-me-nots to face him, with shock registering on her face.

'Because you think if you do you'll be too vulnerable—too afraid I'll run off with some other woman and take Justine with me? Isn't that what your own father kept threatening he was going to do with you?'

She gave a small, pained gasp at his so accurate deduction. Her father had used her as a pawn to keep his wife tolerant of his extra-marital affairs, never knowing the effect it had produced in his daughter or the nightmares she had suffered because of it. Nightmares from which she had always awoken sobbing, she remembered painfully, wondering whether her mother had told Cameron about that, or whether he'd simply guessed.

'But that's just what you said you'd do,' she reminded him in a small, choked voice.

'And you believed me?' Incredulity tinged his words, though not a small amount of self-reproach too. 'Do you really think I'd have been that heartless? For heaven's sake!' Almost angrily he pulled her in front of him. 'Can't you realise I love you, Nadine? I was so desperate to make you mine I would have threatened anything. That's the effect you have on me—had,' he interjected wryly, 'from the very beginning.'

'But you——' She broke off, flushed and disbelieving, unable to take in what he was suddenly disclosing to her.

'Oh, yes,' he breathed. 'Even as a slip of a girl you had the power to disturb me, but I did my darnedest to ignore it, which was why I was so pig-headed to you sometimes in the office—because I couldn't understand it. You were so shy and reticent—and as far as I was concerned you were far too young. After you'd left, though, and we met sometimes socially through Lisa, I——'

He broke off, and, amazed, Nadine could only guess at what he couldn't bring himself to say. That he might have given in to his reluctant interest in her if Lisa hadn't tricked him into marriage?

'I suppose it was inevitable, but from the first moment I held you in my arms in that hotel I was lost to every other woman but you. I tried to deny it to myself. Even when Lisa was taunting me afterwards, to admit that I wanted you, it was like slitting my own throat—playing the hypocrite and forcing myself to pretend it hadn't happened. And the crazy thing was I still wanted you, even when I thought you were a calculating little schemer just after money. Every time I touched you I hated myself—and you for getting into my blood. But when Lisa died and I found out the truth...' His voice had gentled as absently he plucked the delicate, protective wing of a wistaria flower from the pale sleeve of her jacket. 'I knew I had to have you. I couldn't eat, sleep or think straight for wanting you. I even think Simon was beginning to imagine I was going out of my mind.'

What was it Simon had said? He'd never seen a man so lost in himself? But surely not? she thought, amazed. Not over her?

'I thought that if I could get you to marry me...' He pulled a face as he admitted, 'I know my methods were rather unscrupulous, but I hoped that somehow—eventually—I could get you to feel the same way about me.'

He'd hoped to make *her* feel the same...! A little bubble of joy tried to burst from her, but didn't quite make it. She was baffled, utterly confused.

'But how can you say you love me?' she contended woundedly, looking up at him, forcing herself to face up to something that had caused her such intolerable pain. 'What about your relationship with Rachael? You planned to go away with her,' she reminded him, aggrieved, unable to understand why he'd admitted to loving *her* when the other woman was figuring so strongly in his life. 'And you can't deny it. I even heard you telling her in court that she'd have to go on her own...'

To her surprise he looked—what? Surprised? As though he didn't know what she was talking about? Then suddenly he laughed.

'What I think I said was that she was on her own now. But certainly not to take some clandestine trip that had originally been arranged for two. Rachael had invested in some property with Lisa in Majorca, and the owner of the complex out there was trying to close a very underhanded deal. I sorted out the legality of things with her and she was flying out there that day to finalise the relevant paperwork. She'd arranged to pick up a document I'd been looking into from me before I went into court, and only stayed to sit in on the case because her flight wasn't leaving for a couple of hours. But Rachael is very adequately provided for with a very adequately built boyfriend,' he said drily, confirming what Simon had told her that day in the park.

Beginning now to believe what her heart had for so long been craving to hear, tenderly she caressed the broad line of his shoulder, saying with a little pout, 'That didn't stop her wanting you as well.'

'No. I'm afraid Rachael isn't entirely unlike Lisa was,' he said regretfully. 'But you've got no competition, darling. I'm afraid the feeling was never mutual.'

'But she said you were hers before you met Lisa—that she'd introduced you to her,' she remembered, the joy inside her still not quite able to dispel every doubt.

'Yes, that's true.' He smiled, gently caressing her cheek with the back of his hand. 'But I'd only dated Rachael once or twice—and never seriously. We were never anything more than casual friends.'

And now the tenderness of his touch and that oh, so wonderful smile of his were working to dissolve all the fears and worries she had nurtured over the past months, so that she could see clearly now how Rachael had tried to make her think the worst—even going so far as to imply that Cameron hadn't come home during that snowstorm because he'd spent the night with her. She could see now that Cameron would only have needed casually to mention staying in a hotel for the other girl to have used that knowledge to her advantage, while she, too easily influenced by the disaster of her parents' marriage, had nearly succeeded in destroying her own through unnecessary and very reprehensible suspicion.

'Why did you go to her instead of coming to me first when you came back from France?' she whispered, needing to know if it was true, and yet knowing now that if it was, he would have had good reason.

'She was Lisa's closest relative—next to her mother— and that lady was too distraught at the time to inform anyone. Therefore I made it my business to go and see Rachael myself, but all I wanted was to get back to you. I knew by then why you'd changed your mind about giving up the baby, but not how generous and kind and considerate you were—the sacrifice you were making for your mother and what you were going through because of her at the time. When Tuesday accidentally broke that vase and I found that invoice...' His breath seemed to shudder through him as he pulled her to him. 'My dearest Nadine, I've loved you so much.'

'But you never showed an inkling of it. Why didn't you tell me?' she breathed. When he held her away from him a little, so that he could look at her again, she thought that if he had then all the pain, the doubt, the suspicion, could have been so mercifully spared.

'For the same reason I think that you didn't——' he smiled wryly '—and still haven't told *me*. Pride, I suppose,' he admitted ruefully. 'Fear of rejection. That's why I took you to that hotel today, solely to gauge your reaction. Having the same table was just an added bonus to my plans. I wanted to see you weep, if I had to, to tear an admission out of you. I had nothing to lose, as I felt I was losing you anyway, but you responded so proudly at first that I thought the tables were being turned on me for my sheer audacity in thinking you felt anything for me... I thought that I'd been wrong.'

'Oh, no, no, my love, you weren't wrong!' Sensing the desperation he had felt like a palpable thing, she laid her head against his shoulder, her arms inside his jacket, revelling in the warm, wonderful strength of him through his shirt. 'That's why I came to see you at the court that day—to tell you *I'd* been wrong, to try and put things right between us before you went away. I was so frightened you weren't ever going to come back.

'You said in the hospital that you didn't know how you kept from ringing me after that weekend we went away together, and I think some of that must have been because I was willing you to, because I loved you then. I've loved you since that day you first came into the office and flayed me for that mix-up over a hearing that wasn't really my fault. Anyway, after our weekend I felt so guilty because you were married, and I knew I shouldn't have been hurt but I was, because I thought it hadn't affected you in the least. I was prepared to tell you all that the day Justine was born, but then I saw Rachael sitting in the court, and you looked at me as though you didn't even know me.'

Cameron chuckled, stroking her fiery hair, asserting claim over a gustily teasing breeze. 'My dearest, if there's one thing you haven't learned yet about barristers it's that we have to be able to put on a performance as believable as any actor's. In my case that day I had to give everything I'd got to keep myself from seizing up altogether, because when I looked up and saw you sitting there in that gallery I nearly forgot what I was doing— let alone saying!'

'I'm sorry,' she whispered, biting her lip to stem a smile. It had been determined little Justine who had eventually made certain that she wasn't ignored.

'Don't be,' he murmured dismissively. 'All that matters now is that we look ahead. To the future.' Gently his lips brushed her cheek. 'Talking of which...' He separated them, only to take her hand, turning her towards the house. 'I didn't want you to have to face the upheaval of a move until after Justine was born, but do you think you could live here quite happily with me?'

'Anywhere!' she laughed, her eyes shining openly with love for him. 'But I suppose here will have to do.' Delightedly she looked towards the beckoning red brick and the magnolias, and through her joy and excitement the truth suddenly dawned. 'You aren't buying it?' Eagerly she clasped his arm. 'Oh, Cameron! Tell me?' She was almost jumping up and down. 'Is it really going to be ours?'

He laughed at the disbelief in her face. 'I first put a bid in for it back in the autumn, not even knowing if you were going to marry me.'

And he'd kept it a secret from her all this time, she marvelled, saying laughingly, 'But I did!' And, with a bubbling anticipation, 'So when can you take possession?'

He pulled her to him, smiling as they moved towards the house, murmuring in his most seductive tone, 'I thought I already had.'

A little frisson ran through her at the blatancy of his innuendo. Yes, he'd taken possession a long time ago—not just of her body, but of her heart and soul, of every breath she would ever be likely to breathe. But they were meeting on equal terms at last, she thought, smiling up at him as he put the key into the lock. As friends and partners, wife and husband, parents and guardians. As lovers in joint possession—for life.

HARLEQUIN PRESENTS®

**Imagine planning your own
wedding...THREE times!**

Georgia did.

But would the third time be lucky?

**Find out in
#1842 THREE TIMES A BRIDE
by Catherine Spencer**

**Available in October wherever
Harlequin books are sold.**

HARLEQUIN ◆ PRESENTS®

For your eyes only!

Dear Reader,

re: SWEET SINNER by Diana Hamilton
   Harlequin Presents #1841

Zoe's boss, James, had formed the worst
possible impression of Zoe and branded her a
heartless tramp. Could she ever convince him
that he was *so* wrong?

Yours sincerely,

The Editor at Harlequin Mills & Boon

P.S. Harlequin Presents—the best has just
    gotten better! Available in October
    wherever Harlequin books are sold.

P.P.S. Look us up on-line at: http://www.romance.net

HARLEQUIN®

Don't miss these Harlequin favorites by some of our most distinguished authors!
And now, you can receive a discount by ordering two or more titles!

HT #25663	THE LAWMAN by Vicki Lewis Thompson	$3.25 U.S. ☐/$3.75 CAN. ☐
HP #11788	THE SISTER SWAP by Susan Napier	$3.25 U.S. ☐/$3.75 CAN. ☐
HR #03293	THE MAN WHO CAME FOR CHRISTMAS by Bethany Campbell	$2.99 U.S. ☐/$3.50 CAN. ☐
HS #70667	FATHERS & OTHER STRANGERS by Evelyn Crowe	$3.75 U.S. ☐/$4.25 CAN. ☐
HI #22198	MURDER BY THE BOOK by Margaret St. George	$2.89 ☐
HAR #16520	THE ADVENTURESS by M.J. Rodgers	$3.50 U.S. ☐/$3.99 CAN. ☐
HH #28885	DESERT ROGUE by Erin Yorke	$4.50 U.S. ☐/$4.99 CAN. ☐

(limited quantities available on certain titles)

	AMOUNT	$
DEDUCT:	**10% DISCOUNT FOR 2+ BOOKS**	$
ADD:	**POSTAGE & HANDLING**	$
	($1.00 for one book, 50¢ for each additional)	
	APPLICABLE TAXES**	$_____
	TOTAL PAYABLE	$_____
	(check or money order—please do not send cash)	

To order, complete this form and send it, along with a check or money order for the total above, payable to Harlequin Books, to: **In the U.S.:** 3010 Walden Avenue, P.O. Box 9047, Buffalo, NY 14269-9047; **In Canada:** P.O. Box 613, Fort Erie, Ontario, L2A 5X3.

Name: _____

Address: _____ City: _____

State/Prov.: _____ Zip/Postal Code: _____

**New York residents remit applicable sales taxes.
  Canadian residents remit applicable GST and provincial taxes.   HBACK-JS3

Look us up on-line at: http://www.romance.net